How do you say

… "Listen Elsa, we

Elsa thrust out he

Elsa glanced at her bare wrist. "Yup, that's it, right on the nose. It's time for the 'I'm-too-old-for-an-imaginary-friend' speech. Um, I've heard it."

I bent down and started unlocking my bike. "Okay, I know we've talked about this before but I've really been thinking about this a lot lately and …"

Elsa pretended not to be listening. She took a giant pink bubble out of her mouth and started poking it with her finger.

"It's just that I'm turning thirteen this summer and no one has an imaginary friend at thirteen." I put the bike lock in my pack …

"Okay, I just want to remind you that if I go you won't have a shoulder to cry on when you don't get invited to a sleepover, or you don't win a race, or Mr. Bianchini doesn't notice you, or your mom does that thing where …"

"I'm aware of all that!" I yelled.

"And who's going to help you put curses on Ginny Germain?"

"I'll manage. They never work anyway."

"And what about fashion tips …"

"Stop it!" I tried to sound firm …

"Fine." Now she was really mad. Two vertical creases appeared between her eyebrows and her eyes narrowed. "But don't come crying to me when you suddenly realize that I'm the best thing that ever happened to you …"

And then she was gone.

Still There, Clare

Raincoast Books gratefully acknowledges the financial support of the Province of British Columbia through the BC Arts Council and the Book Publishing Tax Credit and the Government of Canada through the Canada Council for the Arts and the Book Publishing Industry Development Program (BPIDP).

Editor: Lynn Henry / Tonya Martin
Cover and interior design: Five Seventeen
Cover illustration by Terry Wong

LIBRARY AND ARCHIVES CANADA CATALOGUING IN PUBLICATION

Prinz, Yvonne

Still there, Clare / Yvonne Prinz.

ISBN 13: 978-1-55192-828-9
ISBN 10: 1-55192-828-0

I. Title.

PS8631.R45S74 2008   JC813'.6   C2007-904850-1

Library of Congress Control Number: 2007933932

Raincoast Books	*In the United States:*
9050 Shaughnessy Street	Publishers Group West
Vancouver, British Columbia	1700 Fourth Street
Canada v6p 6e5	Berkeley, California
www.raincoast.com	94710

Raincoast Books is committed to protecting the environment and to the responsible use of natural resources. We are working with suppliers and printers to phase out our use of paper produced from ancient forests. This book is printed with vegetable-based inks on 100% ancient-forest-free, 100% post-consumer recycled, processed chlorine- and acid-free paper. For further information, visit our website at www.raincoast.com/publishing/.

Printed in Canada by Marquis

10   9   8   7   6   5   4   3   2   1

Still There, Clare

BOOK ONE IN
THE CLARE SERIES
BY

Yvonne Prinz

RAINCOAST BOOKS

Vancouver

For the children of Iraq,
with a wish for peace

Acknowledgements

Merci: To Alex for a chapter a week (no excuses); Linda Coffey for wisely advising me never to tear the fort down (unless your brother poops in it); Karen Masterson and Lori Katz for unconditional girlfriendship and support; my editor Lynn Henry, Michelle Benjamin, Emiko Morita and Jesse Finkelstein for reading Clare and getting her; the Ladies of the Chorus for endless inspiration and belly laughs; Sarah Cooper and the Saint Girls for putting the pieces of the puzzle together; Jenny for finding her way back; Dave for making it all worthwhile.

Chapter 1

"Psst, Clare."

I turned around in my desk. Margaret, who sits behind me in class, handed me a folded note. It said **PRIVATE** in big red letters. You'd think it contained the key to ending world hunger or a cure for AIDS.

"Pass it!" she hissed.

As if I would actually read it! Tiffany, who sits in front of me, and Margaret are best friends. They used to be attached at the head until all the giggling and pointing finally got to Miss Khemlani, our Homeroom teacher and the most patient person in the world. I was the lucky person chosen to sit between them. Now my job is to keep the lines of top-secret communication flowing smoothly. It's almost as fun as it sounds. I tapped Tiffany on the shoulder and gave her the note.

"Thanks," she chirped, snatching it out of my hand with her bright red fingernails.

I watched the second hand creep in slow motion past the big black twelve on the clock above the door. Another minute ticked by. Seven minutes until school was out for the weekend. I looked around the classroom. Everyone was either glued to the clock or amusing themselves somehow. Sam Stern, the class bully, who sits behind Bernard Roseman, the class genius, had a catapult rigged on his desk to fling bits of eraser at the back of Bernard's head. Bernard, who endures abuse from Sam daily, was doing his best to ignore it. Jody, who sits behind Sam, was carefully sewing her fingers together with a needle and thread. Brady, who sits behind Jody, was picking at a scab on his elbow with the intensity of a brain surgeon.

The smell of pure summer, a combination of freshly cut grass and cool, mushroomy dirt, drifted in through all six open windows, torturing us as Mr. Winters droned on about acute angles and parallelograms. The only math anyone was interested in was counting down the minutes. In fact, the only thing anyone in this school really cared about after June first, which happened to be today, was how many days were left until school was out for the summer. I may end up with a "C" in this class but I know the answer to that: twenty-seven.

I tried to concentrate on what Mr. Winters was saying but all I heard was a jumble of blah blah blah, isosceles, blah blah blah, right angle. Poor Mr. Winters, he's the only teacher at our junior high school without a homeroom so he's forced to wander from class to class with a worn-out leather briefcase full of math stuff. To make matters worse, whenever I look at Mr. Winters my eyes seem to drift up to the top of his head, which is bald except for a few hairs hanging on for dear life. The part with no hair is really shiny which makes it even harder not to stare. One time I discussed this with my mom and she said I should try really hard not to stare because it's very traumatic for a man to lose his hair. Especially a young, attractive man like Mr. Winters. Attractive? Puhleese! She must be joking. I may be only twelve but I've got a pretty good idea who's attractive and who's not. Mr. Winters is nice but I don't think any of the girls at this school daydream about his knack for long division or anything.

I looked out the window at the schoolyard as Mr. Bianchini, our P.E. teacher, rounded up a group of boys in green-and-white uniforms on the soccer field and headed toward the red brick gymnasium. The boys passed a soccer ball back and forth between them. Mr. Bianchini is an excellent example of what I mean by attractive. He has black, curly hair that is always sort of messy, and a scar on his chin that only makes him more interesting. He wears gym shorts all the time, even in winter, and he has a crooked smile that makes my heart skip a beat. I think I'm in love with Mr. Bianchini.

Unfortunately, every girl in my school feels the same way I do about Mr. Bianchini, so I really don't stand a chance. I'm easily the tallest girl in my grade and I have long skinny legs that operate independently of each other. I'm also absolutely flat-chested. Bernard Roseman has bigger breasts than I do. I don't even wear a bra! Last fall when school started, all the seventh-grade girls showed up wearing bras. They should really put out a newsletter or something. Audrey Jones, a girl in my P.E. class, looked at my chest while we were changing and said, "I see there have been no new developments over the summer, Clare."

You can imagine how mortified I was but I wasn't about to show up the next day in a training bra. The school year is almost over now and I've made it this far pretending I don't care even though I'd give my entire college fund for even the slightest sign of a chest.

I tuned back in to Mr. Winters for a second. He seemed to be trying to wrap it up but his passion for geometry was getting the better of him. My mind drifted as I stared out the window again, soft-focusing on Mr. Bianchini.

The only time Mr. Bianchini knows I'm alive is when we do track and field in P.E. I'm a pretty good runner and my best event is the 800 metres. I guess it's the long legs. My downfall is a girl named Ginny Germain. She's a better runner than I am, plus she has all her stuff in the right places, if you know what I mean. She's also the most popular girl in school. As if that weren't enough, her brother's also a professional hockey player. Sometimes, when Ginny's out sick or something, I can feel Mr. Bianchini's eyes on me as I cross the finish line ahead of all the other girls. He looks at his stopwatch and gives me that crooked smile. This is a magic moment for me and it keeps me going until it happens again. I live for these moments. I spend way too much time thinking about Mr. Bianchini.

The buzzer finally sounded at 3:15 p.m., signalling a stampede for the exit doors. On Fridays the school hallways are especially treacherous. Everyone thinks that the weekend starts the moment your foot touches that pavement at the end of the chain-link fence marking school property. Students have been trampled in the rush to get there. It's like the mayhem you might see if someone turned out the lights and pulled the fire alarm at a school assembly. I had to fight against the current to get to my locker, and I barely made it. When I got there, Damon Bales was leaning against the locker, talking to a girl. I had to ask him three times to move. He finally walked off with his arm around the girl's waist, ignoring me. The story of my life. Within seconds I found myself standing alone in an empty hallway. I was in no particular hurry. I wasn't looking forward to my weekend. Even though I was mere steps away from a perfect summer day and even though Aunt Rusty and I were going to the beach on Sunday, an event I'd normally be pretty excited about, on this particular Friday afternoon I had to do something that I was dreading; I had to say goodbye to Elsa.

Chapter 2

On the way to the bike racks I saw Ginny Germain standing in the parking lot talking to some guy on a motorcycle. She kept flipping her shiny black hair over her shoulder and laughing as though he were some kind of comedian or something. Ginny is in a whole different category from all the other seventh-grade girls; not only does she get boyfriends who are in eighth grade at our school, she also imports exotic boyfriends from other schools. All this, plus she's a great athlete. I even heard a rumour that she carries condoms in her backpack. Condoms! The most exciting thing in my backpack is watermelon-flavoured lip balm. It's hard not to hate Ginny Germain. I hate her.

I continued through the empty schoolyard. Just past the swings, I saw Elsa leaning up against the empty metal bike racks waiting for me. She was wearing a pair of hip-hugging jeans and a white T-shirt that said EVE WAS FRAMED. She was twirling a piece of bubble gum around her index finger.

"Hi," I said, as I approached her.

"Hi, yourself." She stuck her gum back in her mouth. "You're late."

"Am not; I came right here."

"Everyone else is already gone," she said. "Even those pesky hall monitors."

"So what?" I swallowed hard. "Listen Elsa, we have to talk."

Elsa thrust out her chin, "Let me just look at my watch." Elsa glanced at her bare wrist. "Yup, that's it, right on the nose. It's time for the 'I'm-too-old-for-an-imaginary-friend' speech. Um, I've heard it."

I bent down and started unlocking my bike. "Okay, I know we've talked about this before but I've really been thinking about this a lot lately and ..."

Elsa pretended not to be listening. She took a giant pink bubble out of her mouth and started poking it with her finger.

"It's just that I'm turning thirteen this summer and no one has an imaginary friend at thirteen." I put the bike lock in my pack.

"Remember when we were seven?" Elsa asked, returning the gum to her mouth. "I miss seven. We never had to have these talks back then. And besides, what does age have to do with anything, anyway?" Elsa put her hands on her hips. "I think this maturity stuff is all crap."

"I mean it this time. I'm not going to change my mind." I got on my bike and started pedalling up the hill away from school. Elsa jumped on my handlebars like she's been doing since first grade. I kept pedalling and tried to ignore her, which was agonizing since this was my favourite part of the school day, the part where I unload onto Elsa everything that went wrong and she somehow makes it all seem okay.

"Okay, I just want to remind you that if I go you won't have a shoulder to cry on when you don't get invited to a sleepover, or you don't win a race, or Mr. Bianchini doesn't notice you, or your mom does that thing where …"

"I'm aware of all that!" I yelled.

"And who's going to help you put curses on Ginny Germain?"

"I'll manage. They never work anyway."

"And what about fashion tips? You definitely need help in this department. I shudder to think what you'll wear."

"Stop it!" I tried to sound firm. "It's not that I don't appreciate your friendship, it's just that I have to start thinking about my future. If you don't leave now you might never leave and I'll be this seventy-year-old woman walking around talking to myself."

"Haven't you ever noticed that old people talk to themselves? How do you know they're not talking to their imaginary friends?" Elsa pointed to the sidewalk, where an elderly man was walking his dachshund. "See, his lips are moving."

"He's talking to his dog," I said.

"Or is he?" Elsa smiled her wicked, irresistible smile but I looked away.

"Elsa."

"Fine. Okay. Have it your way. How about if I leave next week? Next week is good for me. I checked my Blackberry and I'm wide open."

"Today, Elsa, it has to be today."

"Fine." Now she was really mad. Two vertical creases appeared between her eyebrows and her eyes narrowed. "But don't come crying to me when you suddenly realize that I'm the best thing that ever happened to you. I'm the only real friend you ever had."

And then she was gone.

I tried to block all thoughts of Elsa as I pedalled right on Maple, which is lined with (you guessed it) maple trees. By the time I turned right on Oak (ditto on the trees) I had tears in my eyes. Elsa had been my best friend for as long as I could remember, and worse, she was my only girlfriend in school and out. I'd always used her as an excuse not to make real friends and I wouldn't have that excuse anymore. I wiped my eyes with the sleeve of my sweatshirt as I passed two boys from my school throwing a football on their front lawn. I concentrated on keeping my bike on the road.

I finally reached our house at the end of Birch Street. It's a drafty, creaky, old blue Victorian where we've been living since I was four. My mom apparently jumped on it and practically stole it after reading in the obituaries that the ninety-year-old woman who owned it originally had died leaving no survivors. She even went to the funeral. Have I mentioned that my mom *was* a lawyer?

My mom likes to tell people that the house has character to spare, which means it's haunted. I'm pretty sure the old woman died in the house. Elsa and I have heard her plenty of times, rattling around late at night moaning about something or other. I'm sure she'd like to get her bony hands around my mom's neck.

I left my bike on the lawn and ran into the house. I snuck in the front door and wiped my face. I didn't want my mom to see me crying. As far as she knows, Elsa's been gone since I was six. The only person who knows the truth is Aunt Rusty and she's sworn to secrecy. I heard my mom in the kitchen and I could smell banana bread baking. Ever since she quit her job as a lawyer six months ago she's been auditioning for the role of Super Mom. She seems to be trying to make up for lost time. I think she follows the other moms around the supermarket and buys whatever they buy. Our kitchen is full of cookbooks, and the fridge, which used to be empty except for pizza boxes and Chinese takeout cartons, is now full of ingredients. My mom watches the Food Channel around the clock on a tiny TV that sits on the countertop.

I heard Julia Child explaining how to truss a duck as I quietly climbed the carpeted stairs two at a time, avoiding the creaks, and made it to my room without my mom hearing me. I flopped onto my bed and cried into my Spider-Man pillowcase. I knew I was behaving like a big baby but I didn't care. When I finally sat up Elsa was sitting next to me on the bed snapping her gum. Her arms were crossed and she was shaking her head.

"You're pathetic. Look at you, wallowing in self-pity. You can't last fifteen minutes without me."

I wiped my eyes again. "I know."

"Listen, Clare, I've been giving this a lot of thought and I think I have an idea."

"You do?" I sniffed.

Elsa stood up and started pacing back and forth on the blue carpet. We used to pretend that the carpet was an alligator-infested swamp. You couldn't touch it with even a toe or you would get eaten. We made rocks out of my stuffed toys and hopped from one to the other.

"Suppose I just went away for the summer?" Elsa asked slowly. "Sort of a trial thing. That way you could write to me, we could keep in touch."

"Where would you go?" I asked, wiping my nose on my sleeve.

"Hmm," Elsa tapped her chin with her index finger. "Europe, definitely Europe. Grab the atlas and let's pick a place."

I pulled the heavy atlas out from under the bed. Elsa and I had spent hours looking at it and dreaming of all the exotic places we would go one day. I flipped the dog eared pages to the continent of Europe.

"Okay," said Elsa, "here's how we'll do it. Close your eyes and point to a place."

I pointed.

"What is it?"

"Oslo, Norway," I said.

"Ugh, no way. Pick again, lower."

I pointed again and opened my eyes.

"Well?"

"It's in France. It starts with a 'V.' I don't think I can pronounce it."

"What's it near?"

I looked at the map. "It's about an inch from Paris."

"Then Paris it is." Elsa suddenly looked dreamy. "Ah, Paris, the Champs-Élysées, the Louvre, Versailles, the Eiffel Tower, French pastry, French pastry, French pastry ... you know, I've never summered in Paris before."

"Elsa, you've never summered anywhere before, except for that time we went to Girl Guide Camp."

"Ah, *oui, mademoiselle*, talk about *Les Misérables*."

I took a red felt pen out of my desk drawer and drew a large circle around Paris. When I looked up Elsa was standing in front of my full-length mirror adjusting a navy wool beret on her head. She was wearing a beige trench coat. She tucked her long blonde hair behind her ears, which made her ears stick out a little.

"There. How's that?" she asked, turning to me.

"Perfect," I said. "You look beautiful."

"Well then, I guess this is *au revoir*. I have a frightfully long trip ahead of me. Of course I am travelling first class. Coach is just so pedestrian." She cocked her head and gave me her most sophisticated look.

"When will you be back?" I asked.

She shrugged. "We'll see. Wasn't that the deal? Remember, Clare, it was your idea in the first place."

She was right. I had no choice but to stick with the plan. I was just surprised at this sudden burst of practicality on her part and I wanted desperately to go with her.

"Goodbye, Elsa," I said, mustering up some false courage. "Have a great trip!"

I sat alone on my bed and tried to look at the bright side. I would still be talking to Elsa, it would just be a little more work. It didn't seem like the end of the world anymore. Besides, it wasn't like I didn't have any friends at all. There was always Paul.

Chapter 3

"Okay, next category," I said, stirring my root-beer float with a straw.

"Ummm, let's see, okay I've got it. Best sci-fi." Paul pushed his glasses up his nose.

"That's easy," I said. "*Blade Runner*, the director's cut. Top that, smarty pants." I tapped my straw on the pink Formica table.

"Top that? *Blade Runner* isn't even technically a sci-fi film!"

"Is, too!"

"It isn't even in the same league as *Zardoz*."

"Here we go with *Zardoz* again. Get over it!" I noisily drained my root-beer float. Paul watched me in disgust. He never drinks floats. All he ever gets at the Dairy Delite, our number one meeting spot, is Coke, no ice. If someone accidentally puts ice in it, he makes them pour him a new one. Weird.

I've been coming here since I was a kid and they have the same pink-vinyl booths they had when I was four years old and I ordered my first root-beer float. Elsa had been sitting across from me where Paul sat right now. Elsa approves wholeheartedly of root-beer floats. She says the person who invented them should probably get a Nobel Prize. Also the person who invented corn dogs, and the machine that swirls chocolate and vanilla soft-serve ice cream into the same cone.

The same guy has owned the Dairy Delite forever. His name is Tiny, which is someone's idea of a cruel joke because he weighs about three hundred pounds. His four kids, who are also (not surprisingly) on the plump side, worked their way through college flipping burgers and serving ice cream here, and now even some of their kids work here, too. I almost feel like part of the family. If the Dairy Delite ever closed I'd probably have to leave town.

Paul was indignant. "How can you possibly compare *Blade Runner* with *Zardoz*? They're not even in the same league. *Blade Runner* was produced for the mindless masses. *Zardoz* is a thinking man's film."

"Two words," I said. "Harrison Ford."

"What's wrong with Sean Connery?"

"He's about a hundred years old! And besides, Harrison Ford is more my type." I chewed my straw and looked at Paul matter-of-factly.

Paul looked at me in disbelief. "So this is your new standard for rating films, whether or not the leading man is your type? Don't you think that's a bit shallow?"

"I am not shallow. If I was I'd be watching Arnold Schwarzenegger movies. I hate Arnold Schwarzenegger movies."

"I know that. I just never knew it was because Arnold's not your type."

Paul has this infuriating gift for arguing that makes me want to kill him almost all the time. I stabbed his hand with my straw. He yanked it away.

"Ow! I was just kidding." He rubbed his hand. "Tell me something. How can you love Japanese monster movies so much when they don't even have a leading man? Don't tell me Godzilla is your type."

"No. I love them with a whole different part of my brain."

"I see." Paul smirked. He bent over and picked up a toy car that had rolled into his foot. He dangled it by its string, contemplating it for a moment.

"You're not going to eat that, are you?" I asked. Paul glared at me and handed it to the kid sitting in the booth behind us.

"Oh, that reminds me, *War of the Gargantuas* is playing at the Princess tomorrow afternoon. Do you want to go?"

"Shoot, I can't."

"I am talking about the place that serves coffee ice cream at the snack bar."

"I know, I know. I'm spending the day with Aunt Rusty."

"Aunt Rusty? She's out of prison?"

"Very funny. I happen to know that tomorrow's going to be a beautiful day and I'll be at the beach while you sit in a dark, gloomy movie theatre by yourself."

"I don't care. My skin can't take the sun and besides, today is a beautiful day and we're just sitting in here arguing."

He had a point. I looked outside at the people passing by, enjoying the day, and I suddenly missed Elsa desperately.

Paul's a decent friend but we aren't that close, nothing like Elsa and me. Paul is a year older than I am and he goes to a private boys' school. He has to take the bus an hour each way. He used to go to my school but his dad made him transfer so that he could get a "proper" education. It's probably just as well. Paul got the tar knocked out of him on a regular basis at public school. His parents are divorced and he lives with his mom but his dad still tells him what to do. Paul's dad is the kind of man who collects war memorabilia like it's fine china. Paul says he has a display case full of grenades and guns and helmets. Paul doesn't like his dad very much. Neither do I.

"Why are you so petulant today?" Paul interrupted my thoughts.

"I am not pestilent!" I said.

"Petulant. I said petulant, but come to think of it, you're both."

"Whatever." Paul is a walking dictionary and I'm constantly being called words I don't know. I waited for him to drop it.

Paul launched into a story about a science experiment that blew up at school and how he couldn't believe that a student had actually mixed a chemical I'd never heard of with another chemical I'd never heard of without first adding another chemical I'd never heard of; I mean, only an idiot wouldn't know that the results would be disastrous. I was only half listening because Todd Marks had just walked in the door of the Dairy Delite. I watched him over Paul's right shoulder as he scanned the room to see if there was anyone there he knew. Todd Marks is in eleventh grade. Everyone knows who he is because he's a really good football player. Around here that will pretty much get you anything. He has all kinds of girlfriends, mostly the cheerleader type. I have to admit he's pretty good looking even though his mouth is always hanging open.

"So then she turned bright purple and her head started spinning around just like in *The Exorcist*."

I focused on Paul. "I'm sorry, what? Somebody's head was spinning around?"

"Just checking. I thought I'd lost you there." Paul continued with his story, "I grabbed the fire extinguisher ..."

I glanced at Todd again. He was leaning against the wall with his arms crossed over his broad chest, waiting for his order. How come I can never manage to look that casual? He caught my eye and I felt my face reddening.

Paul stopped talking and glanced over his shoulder to see what I was looking at. He turned back to me.

"What part of your brain do you love Todd Marks with?" he asked.

"Don't be stupid." I blushed even more deeply.

"Why, Clare, I believe you're blushing."

I quickly looked out the window. "I am not. It's just hot in here."

"It's air conditioned in here," said Paul, "and, by the way, Todd Marks has a brain the size of a Cheerio."

"I know that. But he is pretty cute."

"Sure," said Paul. "If you like cavemen. Don't tell me he's your type!"

"Ugh, of course not! But what do you have against him?" I couldn't quite believe that I was defending Todd Marks.

"He used to pay me to do his Science homework. Elementary science!"

"Well then, you should be nicer to him. He's a client."

"Clare, the guy's a mouth-breathing waste of oxygen."

"Well, he's pretty important to the team," I said.

"Team? What team?"

"The football team!" I said impatiently, as though I were a cheerleader or had actually been to a football game.

"Oh. I didn't think you meant the debate team."

"You're just jealous," I said. I sat back and crossed my arms.

"Of what?" asked Paul.

"Well, for one thing, girls throw themselves at Todd Marks all the time. How many girls have thrown themselves at you? Hmmm, let's see." I looked up at the ceiling and scratched my head. "I guess the answer to that would be a grand total of zero!" I looked at Paul smugly.

Paul's face fell and suddenly I couldn't believe I'd said that to him. How could I be so cruel? Paul's never had a girlfriend but I've never had a boyfriend either. It was mean to shove the truth in his face like that. He's supposed to be my friend.

Paul stood up. "I just remembered, I have something I have to do this afternoon."

"Wait!" I said. "I was just fooling around."

"I think I liked you better when you didn't have a type," he said, and walked stiffly out of the Dairy Delite, letting the door swing closed behind him. The cheerful bell above the door tinkled, announcing his departure. I pretended to be fascinated by a piece of a french fry on the Formica tabletop for a while and then I looked around to see if anyone had witnessed the scene. A few of the booths were filled with sticky children and their parents but none of them were watching me. Todd Marks was staring straight at me, though, with that dumb look on his face. I pretended I was just leaving anyway. I slid out of the booth and walked past him trying to look perfectly natural. I resisted the urge to punch him in his big, stupid arm and say, "Now look what you've done!"

I walked home alone. I wandered past the dry cleaners, the pet store, the gas station. I knew each one by smell more than sight. This was terrific. In twenty-four hours I'd lost my only two friends. How could I be so dumb?

I stopped at the grocery store on the next corner to buy some licorice whips. I didn't really want them, but licorice whips are a Saturday ritual: Elsa and me, licorice whips and a stack of comic books. We would take them out onto the roof outside my bedroom window. It sounds pretty simple but nothing made me happier.

Of course, the Saturday rituals have changed a bit over the years. When we were eight we started this crazy thing called "Gangster Tea Party." I had this little china tea set with pink and blue flowers on it that I found in the back of my closet. Elsa and I would dress up like high-society ladies in high heels with long dresses and ridiculous hats and long gloves, and pretend we were going to a tea party. My name was Bitsy and she was Blanche. We would sit at my yellow wooden table, all proper and everything, passing the biscuits (Necco wafers or Red Hots) and saying please and thank you, talking to our guests (teddy bears and rag dolls) about the weather and garden clubs and where everyone was summering. Suddenly I would pull a plastic machine gun out of my handbag and start shooting. Elsa would flip over backwards in her chair and take cover, pulling out a water pistol and returning fire. Crockery and furniture would fly everywhere, the table would flip over and we would trade gunfire until one of us would go down, blood spraying, legs twitching. The more dramatic the better. Fortunately, our guests only sustained minor injuries so they could always come back the next week. "Gangster Tea Party" fizzled out when no amount of crazy glue could put the tea set back together.

At the grocery store I grabbed some licorice whips and headed for the checkout. Then I spied Mr. Bianchini in the produce section filling a plastic bag with apples. I ducked behind the magazines and hid the licorice behind some TV guides. Suddenly they seemed like a bad idea. The clerk watched me suspiciously as I edged out of the store with my head down. I longed for my bike but it was at home with another flat tire. I thought about Elsa and how she would make me laugh right about now. Not just about the

Mr. Bianchini encounter, but about everything. I picked up the pace. I had to get home and write a letter.

At home my mom had left a note under a magnet on the fridge saying that she was at the supermarket. She was probably out of bananas. I went upstairs to my room and sat at my wooden desk. I pulled out some paper and a pen from the drawer.

Dear Elsa,

Hope you had a good flight. How is Paris so far? My life has been a disaster since you left. I seem determined to destroy what's left of my pathetic friendships by embarking on a self-destructive rampage. Paul is mad at me because I insulted him at the Dairy Delite. He stormed out and left me sitting there and Todd Marks saw the whole thing. I could die. Why is Paul so sensitive? I have to think of a way to make up with him or I'll spend the entire summer sitting in my room waiting for my breasts to grow. Hope you're having a good time in Paris. Come back if you're not.

Love,

Clare

P.S. Almost ran head-on into Mr. Bianchini at the grocery store. Lucky I saw him first. He was buying apples. Isn't that sweet?

More P.S. Aunt Rusty's coming tomorrow. I pray she doesn't cancel. I need to get out of here for a day.

Chapter 4

I got up early on Sunday morning and climbed out my bedroom window in my Spider-Man pajamas to sit on the roof. My mom was still sleeping but my dad's car wasn't in the driveway, which meant he was already at the office or the gym or something. I love to lay on the roof and stare up at the impossibly blue summer sky and let the morning smells and sounds wash over me. I can actually jump from the roof to an old oak tree and climb around or shimmy down the trunk to the ground, but lately I've been liking the roof. From here I can see the whole neighbourhood laid out in neat little squares. People were starting to emerge from their houses to work in their gardens or wash their cars or walk their dogs. Elsa loved the weekends because it meant lazing around talking. She hated school; she thought it was a big waste of time. By third grade she'd stopped coming to class at all.

Eventually I crawled back inside and dressed in an old white T-shirt and my favourite jeans with a tear in the right knee. My mom keeps trying to throw them in the trash but I find a new secret hiding place for them each week. I promised myself I wouldn't think about Paul or Elsa all day and just to make sure, I decided to pull one hair out of my head every time I did. I would either be bald or in a really good mood by the end of the day. I went downstairs and ate a bowl of cereal while I read a comic book. My mom joined me in her bathrobe with a cup of coffee and the newspaper. A tiny Wolfgang Puck was on TV preparing crepes stuffed with veal, which he kept pronouncing "kwapes stuffed wis vee-o."

Aunt Rusty was supposed to pick me up at 11:00 a.m. but I knew she'd be late because she always is. At about 11:30 a.m., I heard her car choking and sputtering as she pulled up in front of the house. I didn't want to appear anxious so I sat at the top of the stairs and waited. My initials are carved into the old wooden banister right at the spot where I always sit when I'm eavesdropping.

My mom was just going out the door for her daily three-mile run when Aunt Rusty walked in.

"Hi, Angela," said my mom. Angela is Aunt Rusty's real name but everyone's called her Rusty since she was kid because of her long red hair. My mom's always called her Angela.

"Hi," said Aunt Rusty. "Going running?"

My mom ignored the question. I guess it was pretty obvious where she was going since she didn't do too much else in that outfit. Aunt Rusty isn't too familiar with exercise clothing; I don't think she ever exercises. Somehow she manages to stay really thin, though. It drives my mom crazy.

"There's coffee. Want some?" offered my mom.

"Had some, thanks. I was up all night, painting. Where's Dan?"

"Working. Where else would he be?" sighed my mom.

Neither of them said anything for a few seconds.

"So you're working on a new painting?" asked my mom. I could tell she was struggling to find things to talk about.

"Um, yeah, I am."

"What's it called?" asked my mom.

"*Death*. It's just a working title."

My mom cleared her throat, which always means she disapproves. "Isn't that what your last painting was called?"

"No. That one was called *Dying*."

"Oh."

My mom finally called me and I came flying down the stairs and hugged my aunt. She was wearing a black tank top and her black leather jacket that I love and she says I get when she dies.

"Hey, how ya doin'?" she asked.

"Great," I said. It was a lie but I couldn't talk in front of my mom.

"Clare, take a sweater," said my mom.

I looked at her funny because I was already holding one. I kissed her goodbye, and as we were going out the door I heard her quietly telling Aunt Rusty not to smoke in front of me.

We got into Aunt Rusty's tiny red convertible. I squeezed my bag into the tight space behind the seats. As we drove away, Aunt Rusty took her black, wrap-around sunglasses off the top of her head and put them on while

I struggled with my seat belt. The floor under my feet was littered with Tootsie Roll wrappers, takeout coffee cups with bright red lipstick marks on them, and cocktail napkins from places I'd never heard of with writing or pictures drawn on them. Aunt Rusty lit a cigarette with the lighter from the dashboard and exhaled. She said what she always says when she smokes in front of me:

"If I ever catch you doing this, I'll kill you."

"Okay," I said.

"So, tell me about school."

"Are you serious?" I asked.

"Yes. Can't I ask about school?"

"Okay. Well, I'm still wildly popular, still dating Biff, the handsome quarterback, and cheerleading's never been better. I can finally do the splits and smile my dazzling smile at the same time."

"Funny," said Aunt Rusty without laughing. "How's the running?"

"Pretty good. Great, actually, if I could get used to being beat by Ginny Germain all the time."

"Which one is she again?"

"The perfect one. The one with all the boyfriends."

"Oh, right. We hate her. How long till school's out?"

"Three weeks, three days, twenty-two hours, seven minutes, fifty-two seconds."

"Approximately?"

"Yeah."

Aunt Rusty drove through the downtown, past the Dairy Delite. A boy and girl were sitting at the table

Paul and I always sit at. They seemed happy. We turned onto the highway out of town. Aunt Rusty shifted into a higher gear and the wind grabbed at our hair and blew it around.

"How's Paul?" she asked.

"I don't think he's speaking to me." I yanked a hair out of my head. It hurt.

Aunt Rusty took a puff on her cigarette. "Why not?"

"I guess I insulted him. I tried to apologize but he didn't really give me a chance."

"Hmmm, maybe you should let him cool off for a couple of days and try again."

"You think so?" I asked.

"Sure, he's just being difficult. Who else does he have to talk to? At least you have Elsa."

I cleared my throat. "Actually, I have some alarming news about Elsa."

"Really?"

"Yeah. She's sort of … gone," I said. I yanked out another hair.

Aunt Rusty took her eyes off the road to look at me. "Gone?"

"Yes. I sent her away. I mean, she decided to go to Paris, at least for the summer."

"Wow, tough week. What are you going to do next? Go live alone in a lean-to on the side of a mountain?"

"I don't know." My voice was shaking and I felt like crying. I yanked another hair from my head. "I'm miserable."

"Here, have a Tootsie Roll." Aunt Rusty handed me one and opened one for herself. She threw the wrapper on the floor under her feet.

I folded my wrapper in halves until it was too tiny to fold anymore. I watched the farms and pretty little country houses fly by. Normally I make up stories in my head about the people who live in them, inventing incredibly romantic lives for them, but I didn't feel like it today. I sucked on my Tootsie Roll and listened to the music that was playing on Aunt Rusty's car stereo. It was strange drumming with a woman wailing in the background. I guess it must have had some sort of rhythm that only Aunt Rusty could hear because she was tapping her fingers on the steering wheel.

We finally pulled into the packed parking lot at Martin's Beach. It's not actually a real beach. It's a man-made lake with sand around it that was brought in by truck. It's named after the farmer who owns the land. If you didn't know the truth you'd think it was a real lake. There are even fish in it.

We found a spot to park in the shade and took our clothes off at the car because we both had our bathing suits on underneath. Aunt Rusty wore a black bikini, and I wore something with a lot more coverage and a lot less sex appeal. Something you might wear to swim the English Channel. We hauled our stuff along a wooded trail that led to the beach and emerged onto the warm sand where we kicked our shoes off and carried them along the beach to a spot without too many screaming children. We put down our blanket and arranged ourselves with magazines, soda, and sunblock all within reach. Aunt Rusty put layers of sunblock on every inch of her exposed skin. Her complexion is milky white and she wants it to stay that way. I sat on the blanket and watched some kids about my age playing volleyball with a beach ball in the water. They were screaming and laughing and having a good time. Even though I didn't know them I was envious.

Aunt Rusty handed me a soda and we read fashion magazines until we were so hot and sweaty we couldn't stand it. I charged into the sparkling water and plunged in. This early in the season the water is icy and it sucked the air out of my lungs. Aunt Rusty stood at the shore with just her toes in the water. I had to coax her in one inch at a time. Once she got in up to her shoulders I challenged her to a race to the raft at the end of the swimming area. I beat her by a hair. When we got out of the water Aunt Rusty reapplied sun block everywhere and made me put some on, too. We lay on our beach towels and let the sun warm our skin.

Whenever a man walked by, he would stare at Aunt Rusty. She was reading a magazine and didn't seem to notice but I sure did. This one guy walked past us and then turned around and walked back over to us. He smiled at Aunt Rusty. I was invisible to him.

"Excuse me," he said. "Don't I know you from somewhere?"

Aunt Rusty put down the magazine and looked over her sunglasses at him like he was something gross she had just pulled out of her vacuum cleaner.

"I don't think so," she said coldly.

"Oh. Sorry, I guess I confused you with someone else."

"Uh-huh." Aunt Rusty went back to her magazine and the guy walked away. I looked at Aunt Rusty.

"Oh, don't give me that look," she said. "The guy was a worm."

"How do you know?" I asked.

"Because I have a worm detector. I'll get you one when you're older."

I laughed and so did she.

"Did guys always look at you like that?" I asked.

"Like what? Like I'm a piece of meat?"

"No. Like that, like 'Me Tarzan, You Jane.'"

"God, I hope not." She made a face.

"How old were you when you, um, you know ... developed?"

"I don't know. I guess I was about your age."

"Were you the last girl in your class?"

"No. I was the first. It was awful. It sort of happened overnight. One day I was playing softball with the guys like I was one of them and the next day I was carrying my books against my chest so they wouldn't stare at me."

"And then what happened?" I asked.

Aunt Rusty sat up and pulled her long hair into a ponytail. "I dunno, I guess I got used to it, 'cause here I am living happily ever after."

"I'm serious," I said.

"Look, Clare. Don't be in such a hurry to be like everyone else. Being different is really special. You should enjoy it. Growing up will happen to you soon enough and it's really no big deal. The only difference is that you get mail with your name on it, mostly bills, and you have to shave your legs and pay taxes."

Did I mention that my Aunt Rusty is a little cynical?

The late afternoon sun started to dip behind the trees and we decided we'd had enough so we trudged back to the car with wet sand squishing between our toes and jumped around on the pavement in bare feet with towels around us as we changed back into our jeans. Aunt Rusty wanted a milkshake so we stopped at a 24-hour diner on the highway back to town. It advertised an all-day breakfast till 3:00 p.m., which was a little confusing. We ordered big chocolate milkshakes and burgers with french fries that we smothered in ketchup. Our waitress had "Marge" stitched in red on her uniform but Aunt Rusty said that all waitress uniforms come like that and it probably wasn't her real name. There were old road signs all over the wall and the booths were covered in sparkly red vinyl. The only other customer in the diner was a guy with a big moustache sitting at the counter. He was wearing a plaid shirt and cowboy boots, and when he picked up his coffee cup I noticed his hands were calloused and dry. Marge, or whatever her name was, seemed to know him really well. His boots had mud on them and I thought he might even be a real cowboy. When I mentioned it to

Aunt Rusty she turned around to look at him and told me that he came with the place.

I liked the diner and I think Aunt Rusty did, too, because she didn't seem to be in any sort of hurry. She even ordered coffee after we were done eating. We talked a lot about music and movies, and Aunt Rusty got me laughing so hard that chocolate milkshake came out of my nose. When the cheque came, Aunt Rusty left a big tip for Marge. She looked at her watch and said we'd better get going because she'd promised my mom she'd have me home early. It was a school night, after all.

On the way home we were quiet. The sun was hanging low in the sky and I was tired from all the food and fresh air. There was a chill in the car with the top down. I scrunched down in my seat and looked up at the sky. When Aunt Rusty pulled up in front of my house I suddenly felt sad at the prospect of school the next day without Elsa. I asked Aunt Rusty if she was coming in.

"No, I gotta run. Call me next week, okay?"

"Sure."

"Hey, are you gonna be talking to Elsa?"

"No, but we're writing."

"Well, write 'Hi' for me. Okay?"

"Sure."

Aunt Rusty handed me a Tootsie Roll.

"Here, for the road."

I laughed and got out of the car. I stood on the sidewalk and watched her drive away. She lit a cigarette and turned the music up loud as she rounded the corner.

Chapter 5

Dear Elsa,

I went to school without you today. For the first time in my life I felt totally alone. During homeroom morning announcements I pretended that they had just announced that the world was going to end and only the twenty-seven people in my Homeroom class would be left alive. The law stated that I had to choose a best friend from amongst the seventeen girls in my class to spend eternity with or I would be tossed into a pit of molten lava and die a horrible death. It was really hard but I finally settled on Melissa Barnes, even though I know you don't like her. I thought that if I ignored the fact that she brags all the time and wears sweater sets, she probably isn't all that bad. While I was thinking about this, she caught me staring at her and gave me a "What-are-you-staring-at?" look. I was really embarrassed. I decided that I would try to sit with her at lunch and give her some made-up story about why I was staring at her. I spotted her in the cafeteria and walked over to her table with my lunch tray. I was about to sit down next to her when she threw her backpack on the chair and said, "That seat's saved." I pointed to the one across from her and she said, "That's saved, too." She gave me her phoniest smile. As I walked away in search of a giant hole to crawl into, I heard her and her friends laughing at me. I hope Melissa Barnes gets incurable teenage acne. And, just for the record, those sweater sets look really stupid.

I phoned Paul's house when I got home but his mom picked up. She said, "I think he's out with Clare somewhere." I said, "This is Clare," and she said, "Oh. Well then, I don't know." If she was covering for him, she was doing an awful job. The only place Paul could possibly be after school is with me. Hmmm.

I really hope you're having a good time. Aunt Rusty says "Hi." I smell food burning. It must be dinnertime.

Helplessly,

Clare

After I finished writing Elsa, I went downstairs and noticed that my mom had the big farm table in the dining room set for two with cloth napkins, candles and matching napkin rings. I've spent my entire life not even knowing what a napkin ring is and suddenly I'm surrounded by them. Eating in the dining room is an entirely new concept, too. In fact, eating anything that didn't come in a box with a takeout menu taped to it was unheard of until lately. The other night my mom had the napkins folded into cranes, which, it turns out, are birds, not those giant orange things you see at construction sites. Who knew?

In the kitchen my mom was hovering over the stove. She didn't hear me come in because she had a Van Morrison CD turned up loud.

"Hi, Mom!" I yelled.

She jumped. "Geez, Clare, don't sneak up on me like that." She turned down the music with the remote.

"People who are sneaking don't yell things," I said.

"I'm making your favourite dinner," she said, ignoring me. "Cannelloni with tomato sauce. Your dad won't be home until late, so it's just us girls."

My mom likes the term "us girls" quite a bit. She acts like we're in a sorority together or an exclusive club with passwords and secret handshakes. I'm not comfortable with any of it. Most of the time, I feel like we're from different planets. I sat on a stool at the counter and watched her cook. I wondered why she thought cannelloni was my favourite dinner, but I decided not to say anything.

"How was school today?" she asked.

"Great."

"Where's Paul these days?"

"I dunno." I shrugged.

She poured dressing on a salad and tossed it. "You two didn't have a fight, did you?"

"No, not really." I didn't want to tell her what had really happened, and besides — a fight? That's ridiculous. Parents fight, kids disagree.

"That's good. Paul's a nice kid."

Oh, right, I thought. *Since when?* She's always told me that Paul was too sarcastic and a bad influence on me. This liking Paul thing was definitely new. My new, improved mom is just way too understanding. She's trying to play catch-up for all the years she missed when she was a career woman. The first eleven years of my life I went from Pooh Bear's Day Care (aliens) to Applebee's After School Care (fascists) to Noreen, the babysitter (Satan). Sometimes my parents would forget whose turn it was to pick me up so whoever was in charge would have to track them down and remind them that they had a kid. They weren't horrible parents or anything, just really busy.

One time, in second grade, I was an angel in the Christmas pageant at school. All the angels in my class had to bring their costumes home for their moms to sew. My mom was too busy, so the night of the pageant she stapled it together and told me to stand in the back. I felt pretty stupid standing on that stage next to all the other angels in their neatly sewn costumes. I could tell my teacher felt sorry for me.

My mom pulled the cannelloni out of the oven and brought it into the dining room. We sat down and she dished up our salads. I picked the mushrooms out of mine.

"How was yesterday with your Aunt Rusty?" asked my mom.

"Good. We had fun."

"She didn't smoke, did she?"

"Nope."

"Good."

"Mom," I asked, "why do you suppose Aunt Rusty doesn't have a boyfriend?"

She thought about it. "Hmmm, I don't know. I guess she just hasn't found the right guy."

"But she's so pretty," I said.

"Just because you're pretty doesn't mean you're always going to have a boyfriend. Besides, maybe she just doesn't want one right now. I'm sure she meets lots of interesting men in her, um, you know ... work."

I thought about this for a minute. If someone who looks like Aunt Rusty can't find a boyfriend, how was someone who looks like me ever going to? I picked up a spoon and examined my reflection in it. My nose looked enormous and my "constellation" (my mom's word) of freckles looked more like an asteroid attack. At least there were no signs of acne yet (although I kept a tube of emergency Clearasil next to my bed), but my hair was a disaster, kind of a cross between a cocker spaniel and a hamster. Add that to my nonexistent figure and, well, there was always my effervescent personality. The way things were going, I would probably live out my days in a Buddhist monastery on top of a mountain in Tibet.

I cleared away the salad plates and my mom served up the cannelloni. It tasted pretty good, considering it was made by my mom. No one would mistake her for an Italian or anything, but I ate everything she put on my plate and even had seconds. For dessert there was Butter Brickle ice cream, which I happen to love. My mom scooped some into a bowl and set it in front of me. She didn't have any herself because she's always on a diet. She crossed her arms on the table and watched me eat mine. After a while she started spooning ice cream directly out of the carton into her mouth, something she never lets me do. After a few spoonfuls, I could see she was getting close to the bottom.

"Mom," I asked, "aren't you going to save any for Dad?"

"Nope, he hates Butter Brickle."

"No, Mom," I said. "It's Rocky Road he hates. He loves Butter Brickle."

She sighed and looked at the almost empty carton. "I guess I'd better finish now. What he doesn't know won't hurt him, right?"

"Sure, Mom."

After she hid the ice-cream carton under some things in the trash bin, my mom made us cappuccinos on her new espresso machine. She insisted on putting *La Bohème* on the stereo so that our suburban dining room would feel like an Italian café. If there's one thing my mom loves, it's atmosphere. She doesn't usually let me drink coffee, but she loves using her new machine. I think it's foaming the milk she really enjoys. The machine was a gift from her law firm when she quit. She told me she had a six-cappuccino-a-day habit while she was a lawyer. I call that an addiction.

She set my cappuccino down in front of me with a salt shaker full of powdered cocoa. That explained why I couldn't find the salt earlier. I sprinkled chocolate over the foam and took a sip. It left a moustache on my upper lip and I licked it off. My mom did the same, but not before I could laugh at how funny hers looked.

Suddenly, she stopped laughing and got serious.

"Clare, is there anything you'd like to talk to me about?"

I sensed danger. "Like what?" I asked cautiously.

"Oh, I don't know," she stared into her coffee, "school, friends, life, whatever."

"Why?" I asked suspiciously.

"Well, I've noticed lately that you don't have a little group of girlfriends —"

I interrupted. "Lately? You've noticed this lately? Mom, I've never had a little group of girlfriends, you were just too busy to notice!"

"Okay, that's true, but as I was saying, well, Paul seems to be your only friend and —"

"What's wrong with Paul? You just said you liked Paul!"

"I do. I just think that it would be nice if you had some girlfriends, too, that's all."

"Well, I don't, and if you must know, Paul isn't my friend anymore, either."

My mom's timing couldn't have been worse. I started to cry for the second time in three days. I generally only cry during Disney animated movies and long distance telephone commercials. My mom said she was sorry. She said she was only trying to understand me better. She hugged me and I ended up forgiving her. This thing where we say we're sorry and forgive each other is as new as the napkin rings. I wonder who kidnapped my real mother?

I went up to my room early, put on my Spider-Man pajamas, and read my latest manga, a Japanese comic book called *Love Hina, Volume 13*, which I'd bought with Paul at Atomic Comics last week when we were still friends. When I finished reading, I got into bed and hauled the atlas out and looked at the page with France on it and the circle around Paris. I stared at it for a long time, trying to see Elsa, trying to imagine what her life was like down there. I wished that Paul was still my friend so that he could annoy me with a million facts about Paris.

Chapter 6

The next day the most unexpected thing happened. I hadn't run the 800 metres in a while, but we were training for the upcoming track meet. Right at the beginning of the race, I looked over at Ginny Germain, with her shiny black hair and her perfect pointy little nose and her orthodontist-assisted amazing smile, and I was filled with rage. I started thinking about that sixth-grade sock hop when all the boys were asking her to dance and I just stood there against the gymnasium wall trying to look like I didn't care, but praying someone would ask me to dance. Bernard Roseman, the biggest loser in school, spotted me like a heat-seeking missile from across the gymnasium and came lumbering over to answer my prayers. I was mortified. I walked onto the floor with him and it was immediately clear he couldn't dance at all. The frightening thing was that I was only slightly better. Neither one of us had any business being in the middle of the floor without our shoes, surrounded by people watching us. I was praying for an alien abduction. Ginny Germain and her friends were standing around the punch bowl snickering and actually pointing at us. I excused myself and walked off the floor and out of the gymnasium door. I walked around for an hour in my stocking feet and when I came back everyone was gone and the doors were locked with my shoes inside. I had to walk home in my socks. Elsa and I froze a piece of paper with Ginny Germain's name into an ice cube that night, hoping to put a curse on her. We'd learned that from my *Curses for Beginners* book.

I can't explain it, but thinking about that night and feeling that rage made me run so fast I almost threw up when I crossed the finish line. I looked back and Ginny Germain was at least a hundred feet behind me. Mr. Bianchini came right over to me and gave me a high-five. My hand was stinging and it was the only part of my body I could feel for a while. I don't have to tell you how wonderful it felt. The best part about it was that I beat Ginny Germain's personal best by half a second. Ginny was not pleased, and there was a lot of whispering and huddling with her ladies-in-waiting (that group of girls who will do anything for Ginny so that they can be popular by association) after the race.

Maybe the key to getting anything you wanted was just to want it bad enough. I decided to put my theory to work on several other parts of my life immediately. Which meant I would have breasts, a boyfriend and be the most popular girl in school by the weekend. I realized how completely shallow that sounded, but was it wrong to want it just a little? I wished I could ask Elsa.

Right after school, I was still feeling pretty confident, so I marched over to Paul's house and knocked on the door. While I waited for someone to answer the door, it struck me that Paul's house looked like no one lived there. The curtains were drawn and both front doors were shut, which seemed strange for a summer day. The paint on the house was peeling so badly that it was hard to tell what colour it was supposed to be. The front yard was a jungle overgrown with weeds the size of small trees. Paul's mother finally came to the door. She looked like she had just gotten out of bed, except she had a frosty martini in her hand. I asked if Paul was home and for a minute it seemed like she couldn't quite place him. Then she went away and Paul finally appeared at the door. I think I caught him off-guard because he looked really happy to see me, then he remembered he was mad and regarded me coolly.

"Hullo."

"Hi." I acted like nothing had happened. "I was just in the neighbourhood."

"You live in the neighbourhood." He didn't invite me in. He just stood there.

"Well, sure, for now, but we're moving."

"Really?" He tried to look calm but I saw the horror.

"Kidding." I said.

He looked relieved. "Oh."

We stood there in silence for a second. Then I said, "Hey, do you want to go to the Japanese Monster Movie Festival at the Princess on Saturday?"

"Sure, I guess."

So we made up. Who knew it could be so easy? When I told Paul about beating Ginny Germain, he said, "At what?" Okay, so he's not the perfect friend, but he's better than nothing.

Later, after dinner, I went upstairs to write to Elsa with the news of the day. I especially wanted to tell her about a dream I'd had about Mr. Bianchini the night before. I was running a race with hundreds of other girls, and every time I looked at the finish line, it was further away. Mr. Bianchini was standing at the end cheering for me. All of a sudden, I was the only person running and the race was over. I crossed the finish line and Mr. Bianchini swept me into his arms and spun me around in slow motion. We were both smiling. He brought his face close to mine and he seemed about to kiss me when I woke up. My heart was pounding.

As I sat at my desk writing the dream details down, I started to feel a presence over my right shoulder. I turned around in my chair and there stood Elsa, bent over me, watching me write.

"You forgot an 'i' in Bianchini." She pointed to my letter. "Right there."

"What are you doing here?" I asked.

"Um … I forgot a couple of things."

"Like what?" I crossed my arms over my chest.

"Um … my Mickey Mouse ears and those coloured pencils that smell like flowers when you write with them." She avoided my eyes and looked at my bed. "Hey, is that a new duvet cover?"

"Elsa?"

"Oh, all right! I missed you, okay? You sounded so alone in your last letter. I couldn't bear it."

I noticed that Elsa's hair was pulled back tightly like a ballerina's and she was wearing silver hoops in her ears.

"When did you get your ears pierced?"

"Today. Do you like it?" She looked at herself in the mirror and touched one of the hoops.

"Sure, except we were supposed to do it together when we were thirteen, remember?"

"Yeah, but everyone in Paris is so grown up. I didn't want to look like a little girl." She flopped onto my bed and tried to look nonchalant.

I was hurt and a little jealous. And I wanted her to stay forever.

"Can you stay for the night?"

"No, just a while. I have to be in Paris for *petit déjeuner* and it's almost morning there. My friend Guy is giving me a French lesson."

"Guy? Who's Guy?"

"Oh, just a friend. I met him on the Metro."

"How old is this Guy fellow?" I asked, sounding very much like an over-protective mother, mine to be more specific.

"Fourteen." She looked at me coyly.

Twenty minutes in Paris and she already had a social life.

Elsa stayed for an hour that felt like ten minutes, and then she had to go. Before she left, I asked her a question that had been bothering me.

"Elsa, do you think it's wrong to want to be someone else?"

"Of course not," she said, "as long as the person you become is still the person you are." She winked at me and then she was gone.

Chapter 7

It's amazing how just one thing can go right and everything seems to fall into place. Paul and I settled back into our routine of watching sci-fi videos, arguing, reading comic books, arguing, playing Scrabble, arguing, and hanging out at the Dairy Delite, arguing. I have to admit, there were moments when I asked myself if making up with Paul was the right thing to do, especially when he went on for days about the history of mummification. That's when I had to remind myself that an annoying Paul is better than no Paul.

On Saturday, Paul and I went to the Japanese Monster Movie Festival. I got my mom to drop us off nice and early so we could get a good position in line. The popularity of Japanese monster movies is highly underrated. When we got there, we were behind eight people in line and I knew I could outrun most of them. We stood on the sidewalk outside the theatre and read comic books. The line grew longer and longer behind us, snaking past the Vietnamese restaurant, the cigar store, and even the health food store at the end of the block. As soon as the doors opened and our tickets were torn, Paul handed me his stuff and I sprinted for the best seats, dead centre of the theatre, exactly one third of the way back. Paul joined me a little later with a large cardboard tray full of essential movie snacks that included one large popcorn, one large box of juji fruits, one large bag of Twizzlers and two large Cokes (Paul's without ice, of course). Total cost of the snacks: about $375. Total grams of fat: about the same. I reminded myself to do extra push-ups and sit-ups before bed. We settled into the plush velvet seats and arranged our snacks around us for easy access. I inhaled deeply, enjoying the old-theatre smell. It reminded me of the smell of my leather ballet slippers, left over from the three miserable months when I thought that I could become a ballerina. The lights in the theatre slowly faded and the giant velvet curtains parted, revealing the opening credits for *Rodan*.

After several hours of monster-mania, including *Mothra* and *War of the Gargantuas*, we stretched our stiff legs and stumbled out into the street squinting like mice in the bright sunlight. When my mom had dropped us off, she'd told me we could get a ride home from my dad. His office is walking distance from the theatre and Saturday is just another working day for him. My mom made me promise to go directly there, which we did except for two mandatory stops at comic book stores. Paul deliberated forever and finally settled on an *Amazing Spider-Man* double issue after I told him I was leaving without him. It only took me a minute to find what I was looking for: *Nightmares and Fairy Tales*. I'd been waiting for it all month.

When we got to my dad's office building, we played around in the fountain out front for a while. We wanted to see who could fling a penny closest to the metal sculpture

in the centre of the fountain. I won. We went two out of
three. I won again. We entered the giant revolving glass
doors at the front of the building and rode the high-speed
elevators up and down a few times before getting off at
my dad's law office on the twenty-second floor. Miss
Steadman, my dad's personal assistant, looked up from
her desk as we opened the heavy doors to the outer office
and padded across the soft oriental carpet. I hadn't seen
Miss Steadman in a while, but she looked the same as she
always had. She was wearing a dark green, masculine suit
with brass buttons up to her chin. Her hair was pulled back
tightly into a bun. She had the severe, no-nonsense look of
a Doberman pinscher. My mom's always been terrified of
her and I don't blame her. Miss Steadman watches over my
dad like a gargoyle. She never takes a vacation or even a day
off, not even weekends. Creepy. The only feminine thing
about Miss Steadman was a delicate pearl chain around her
neck. It was attached to her reading glasses. I approached
her with caution. I could tell she had no idea who I was.

"May I help you, young lady?" She peered over her tiny
gold glasses at me like the big, bad wolf.

"Miss Steadman, it's me, Clare. I'm here for my dad."

It took a few seconds, but she finally recognized me.

"My goodness, Clare, I had no idea. You've grown so
much!"

Really? I thought. *Tell me something I don't know.*

Paul wandered through a set of glass doors on the left
into the oak-lined law library. Miss Steadman focused a

cautious eye on him as though he might steal one of those stupid law books or something. Then she turned her attention back to me and mustered up her best fake smile.

"You're rather tall for your age, aren't you?" she asked as if she was the first person ever to notice that.

"Yeah, maybe, but I am twelve, almost thirteen, actually."

"Oh, my. I remember when you were a little baby. You were so ..." She paused, "well-behaved." She said it as though I were on parole now. "How time flies," she sighed.

"Yeah, it sure does," I said, wondering if that was enough polite small talk. "So, is my dad around?" I asked.

I heard a crash coming from the library, but I pretended not to notice. Miss Steadman looked alarmed, but quickly composed herself and went back to her thin-lipped smile.

"Your father is very busy today," she said, as though that might surprise me or something. "Is he expecting you?"

"Yes," I tapped my sneaker impatiently. Was she suggesting that I need an appointment to see my own dad?

"He's just finishing up a meeting; I don't imagine he'll be long. Why don't you and your little friend have a seat."

"Sure," I said.

I sank into the overstuffed leather chair next to a potted palm and picked up a magazine, pretending to read. I left Paul to rummage through the library because I knew it was annoying Miss Steadman. The things that interest

Paul amaze me. The law library is as exciting as a paint store to me. Out of the corner of my eye, I saw him pushing himself along the bookcases on a wheeled ladder. He occasionally stopped and pulled out a book and then continued on. Miss Steadman couldn't help herself.

"Is he looking for something specific?" she asked.

I really wasn't sure. "Hey, Paul," I shouted. "What are you looking for?"

Miss Steadman winced.

Paul's voice came out muffled from behind a row of books. "*People versus McLean*, landmark case, nineteen fifty-one. This kid actually poisoned his entire Chemistry class one person at a time with simple everyday lab chemicals. He had nothing against any of them, he just wanted to see if it would work ... hmm, this is sort of interesting, too ..." His voice trailed off.

I smiled at Miss Steadman and snapped my gum. She wasn't amused.

The door to my dad's office finally opened and a tall man in a grey suit with shiny black hair walked out, followed by my dad. They shook hands right in front of me and my dad thanked him. The man nodded to Miss Steadman on the way out. My dad walked right past me on the way back to his office and then backed up. I must have looked vaguely familiar.

"Clare, hi! What are you doing here?" he asked.

"Uh, Dad, the movies, remember? You're supposed to drive us home."

He scratched his head. "Oh right, sure. Let me finish up. I'll just be a minute." He went back into his office and shut the door again. I think my dad would be a lot happier to see me if he could figure out a way to bill me for the time.

Miss Steadman cleared her throat and gave me a look as if to say, "See, you really shouldn't be bothering him." I stared right at her as I blew a giant pink bubble with my gum.

My dad took longer than a minute. He took fifteen endless minutes. I made a mental note to take the bus next time. Paul was still having the time of his life, but I was bored out of my mind and Miss Steadman and I were really sick of looking at each other.

My dad finally emerged, briefcase in one hand, cell phone in the other. We rode the elevator down to the parking garage, leaving Miss Steadman to contemplate kids these days.

On the way home, I rode in the front seat with my dad, and Paul sat in the back, rifling through my dad's law stuff. My dad was on his cell phone the whole way, but I saw him looking in his rearview mirror at Paul from time to time. I could tell he was wondering who this kid was, going through his stuff. He looks at me that way sometimes. When my dad finally got off the phone, he asked Paul if he was interested in law.

"No sir, not really," Paul mumbled.

I turned around and rolled my eyes at him.

When we got to our neighbourhood, my dad quietly asked me where he should drop off my friend.

"Dad, you know where Paul lives," I answered loudly. I looked at him in disbelief.

"Paul? Oh yeah, sure, I remember."

He pulled into Paul's neighbour's driveway, but Paul said that was close enough and got out saying he'd call me. My dad and I drove the rest of the way without speaking. I rolled my window all the way down and inhaled the dinnertime smells in my neighbourhood, mostly the smoky smell of barbecues. I hoped some of it was coming from my house. When we pulled into the driveway, I seized a rare opportunity. Elsa had taught me this: whenever your mom or dad act like less than model parents, make sure you ask them for something you really want.

"Dad, can I have a dog?" I asked.

"A dog?" He looked confused.

"Yeah, you know, four legs, furry."

"Clare, I know what a dog is. Can we please discuss this later?"

"Later later, or never later?" I asked.

"Clare, please."

"Sure," I said. I slammed the car door and went in the house. Elsa's technique only works if you can get the parent to feel guilty. It doesn't work if the parent is oblivious.

Chapter 8

Bonjour Elsa,

Apparently, being a fast runner doesn't exactly shoot you up the popularity ladder unless your name happens to be Ginny Germain. I walked into the girls' bathroom after Math class yesterday and bumped into Alana Steinman, sitting on a sink, apparently holding a board meeting to discuss a guy named Tony from another school. As soon as they saw me they all stopped talking and stared at me. There's nothing quite like peeing with seven people listening to you. I was out of there in about twelve seconds.

The school track meet is looming. I'm feeling stronger every day. I REALLY want to win this race. My mom and I started running together at night. It was her idea. At first I thought it would be awful, another pathetic stab at bringing us closer together. I thought she would give me the third degree every night, but it's actually kind of nice having someone to run with. It takes my mind off the agony.

I daydream about you in Paris all the time, walking down narrow cobblestone streets, stopping in at a sidewalk café for a café crème, wandering around fabulous art museums. I'm working hard on my French and Madame Benoit (a.k.a. Frenchy la Prude) calls on me a lot more in class even though I constantly question the usefulness of phrases like, "My crayon is red" and "My bicycle is yellow." I suggested she teach us phrases like, "Can you direct me to the nearest pastry shop?" and "I'm new in town, would you like to show me around?"

I have to go. My mom's screaming at me to get ready. Speaking of art, we're going to a gallery opening featuring Aunt Rusty's art tonight. Well, actually it's a coffee house, but there's going to be champagne and music. Mom's in a bad mood because I know she doesn't want to go, but she's obligated because Aunt Rusty's her sister and everything. Personally, I can't wait. I just wish I had something wonderful to wear. I guess I'll just wear something understated; I've got a closet full of it. I miss you so much I can't stand it. I hate having to explain myself to people.

So there,
Clare

The coffee house turned out to be in what my mom calls a "sketchy neighbourhood." The streets were lined mostly with warehouses. My mom was nervous about parking and wondered if the car would still be there when we got back, but I assured her it would be protected by the guard dog that was eyeing us like we were dinner from behind a chain-link fence. Our shoes echoed on the deserted pavement as we headed toward the blue neon of the coffee house. Once inside, though, it was warm and bright and alive with people. The scene looked a little like Halloween at a mortuary. Almost everyone was wearing black. There were a lot of tattoos and piercings and chalky white skin. Most of the women (at least I think they were women) wore bright red lipstick. My mom surveyed the scene, turned to me, and said, "Twenty minutes and we're out of here, okay?" Everyone was drinking champagne and milling around in front of Aunt Rusty's enormous paintings. The paintings were very sinister, with swirls of dark colours. The subject of every one of them was a woman who was obviously in some sort of pain. I'd seen a lot of them before, so I wasn't expecting daisies or anything. Seeing them all cleaned up and hung on these high white walls was very exciting.

My mom was anxious to find Aunt Rusty since this wasn't the kind of crowd she felt comfortable in. We finally spotted her talking to a man wearing black leather pants and a black T-shirt; he had a shaved head and an earring in his nose. Aunt Rusty looked beautiful. She was wearing a long, tight-fitting black dress. It made her skin look especially white, like porcelain. She was a shoo-in for president of the Chalky-White-Skin Club that was meeting over by the painting of the naked woman holding a knife over her head. I called to her and she waved us over. She looked really pleased to see us.

"I'm so glad you made it!" she said, hugging both of us at once.

"Don't be ridiculous," said my mom, looking around nervously. "We wouldn't miss it for the world."

Aunt Rusty introduced us to the man she was talking to. "Gavin, this is my sister Beth, and my niece Clare."

We said hi.

"Gavin is the guy who put my show together."

"Oh," said my mom. "It's beautiful."

"Uh-huh," said Gavin, suddenly looking bored. A tall thin girl with a matching nose ring came over and stuck her tongue in his ear. He excused himself and walked away with her. Aunt Rusty led us over to the bar. She didn't ask us what we wanted, she just handed us each a glass of champagne. I almost got a sip before my mom took mine away and gave it to Aunt Rusty. She asked the bartender for 7-Up and he was nice enough to put it in a champagne glass so I could at least pretend.

"Thank God you got here," said Aunt Rusty. "I couldn't stand another minute with that creep."

"Who, Gavin?" asked my mom. "But he seemed so sweet."

Aunt Rusty rolled her eyes. "Very funny."

"Why does everyone here look so ... back from the grave?" asked my mom.

Aunt Rusty shrugged. "What do you mean?"

My mom dropped it. "Well, at least you finally got your own show."

"Yeah, and I'll probably have to give him my first born." Aunt Rusty waved to someone across the room.

"You're having children?" asked my mom sarcastically.

"What's that supposed to mean?" Aunt Rusty asked.

I jumped in before things got ugly.

"Have you sold any paintings?" I asked. Aunt Rusty gulped her champagne and held up two fingers.

"Two paintings? Wow, that's great," I said.

"Uh-huh." Aunt Rusty put her empty glass on the bar and grabbed a full one. "Just in time to pay the rent."

"It's only the middle of the month," said my mom.

"I mean last month's rent," she said.

I knew what my mom was thinking, but thankfully she didn't say a word.

I went looking for the bathroom. On the way I saw a woman in a beige trench coat with a navy beret pulled down low and dark sunglasses. She was sipping a glass of champagne and studying one of the paintings. I was about to walk right past her when I suddenly smelled French perfume. I heard her whisper my name.

"Elsa? Is that you?" I asked.

"Hi, stranger," Elsa said in a husky voice.

"What are you doing here?" I gasped.

"Unfinished business," she said, peering over her glasses at me. Her eyes travelled down to my grey T-shirt and beige corduroys. "What's with the outfit? Honey, grunge is *so* over!"

I looked at the champagne. "Do you think you should be drinking?"

"Definitely. Meet me in the ladies' room."

When I got to the bathroom, she was already there.

She was leaning against the sink with her arms crossed, looking very sophisticated.

"What's with all the mystery?" I asked.

"I wanted to tell you a couple of things," she said.

"Are you coming back?" I asked. "Is that it? Because you know you can't."

"No. I wanted to tell you that I think you're doing fine. Try not to miss me so much, though."

"Is it that obvious?"

"Yup, you're still moping around like Eeyore on a bad day. Of course, that's perfectly understandable." Elsa looked at herself in the mirror and tucked a strand of hair behind her ear. "Oh, and about the track meet."

"Yeah?"

"You have to win that race."

"Why?"

"You just do. Okay?"

"Sure," I said, but I wasn't at all sure.

"Well. I've gotta run; I'm on the red-eye back to Paris."

"Hey, Elsa," I said.

"Yeah."

"Do you still miss me sometimes?"

"Only every minute," she said. "Now get out there and mingle. Shoo!" she waved me out the door with her leather-gloved hand.

Back in the main room, Aunt Rusty introduced us to her friends. They were all a little unusual, but I liked each and every one of them. We met a performance artist named Lulu, two dancers named Zach and Ethiel, a poet named Alex, a cab driver named Bob who didn't know Aunt Rusty but just happened to be driving by, and a sculptor named Ryan who welds things out of old car parts.

My mom and I ended up staying a lot longer than I thought we would. After a while, a jazz band started playing. The music was pretty strange, definitely not the stuff you hear on the light jazz radio station my mom plays in the car. (Aunt Rusty says they should only be allowed to play that stuff in malls and hell.) Everyone was dancing and laughing and having a great time, including my mom. By the time we left, Aunt Rusty was well on her way to selling a third painting and Elsa was on her way back to Paris.

Chapter 9

The next day, after school, Paul and I rode our bikes to the science museum. It's about three miles from my house if you take two shortcuts that we discovered a couple of years ago. You have to go under a bridge, through some woods, and carry your bike up two flights of stairs. Paul hates that part and always remembers to tell me that his bike weighs a lot more than mine. The museum is in a small park. It's a super-modern building made of cold, grey concrete. It looks a bit like a giant army bunker. My mom thinks it's an architectural nightmare, but if she had her way, everything would look like the candy house in *Hansel and Gretel*.

We locked our bikes up outside and walked through the turnstiles. They led to "The World of Electricity," which is dull, dull, dull. We goofed around for a while and then headed over to "Bugs!" (our favourite part of the museum and really the only reason we came).

We peered through the glass at the giant Amazonian tarantula as it contemplated its dinner of unsuspecting crickets and beetles.

"They're very efficient hunters," said Paul. "Certain rainforest tribes worship them. In their own habitat they'll even attack a snake."

"Ugh," I made a face and tapped on the glass, trying to warn a slow-moving beetle. "Run for your life," I said.

"People eat them in the rainforest, you know," said Paul.

"Yuck! What for?"

"They fry them up like crabs and they take the eggs out of the female, roll them in a leaf and cook them like a little omelette."

"Hmmm, do you think they have ketchup in the rainforest?" I asked.

"Doubt it," said Paul.

"There's not enough ketchup in the world to make that taste good."

We stood watching as the giant spider suddenly pounced on the beetle.

"I'm never eating crab again," I said.

We watched in disgust as the spider prepared his snack.

"My dad's sending me away to prep school in the fall," said Paul suddenly. He kept his eyes fixed on the spider as though he were addressing it.

"What?!" I shrieked, turning to face him.

"Quiet." He pointed to the spider. "You'll scare him."

"I'll scare HIM? What do you mean, prep school … why?"

"I dunno, it's all part of this obsession he has with getting me a proper education. He's not going to be happy until I'm wearing a uniform; I'm just lucky he's not sending me to a military academy. You know how much he loves guns."

A group of children were trying to get a look at the spider as it did unspeakable things to the beetle. We moved on to the next display: an ant farm.

I realized I'd been a little preoccupied all day with what Elsa had told me at the art show. That thing about having to win the race. Why was it so important to her? I guess I hadn't noticed that Paul was acting strangely, but now that I thought about it, he'd been awfully quiet all afternoon.

"I'm assuming, by the way you're breaking this to me, that this school isn't exactly around the corner."

"No. It's in the East. The glossy brochure mentions rolling hills and breathtaking views."

"You mean like a cemetery?" I mused.

"Exactly."

"Paul, you have to change your dad's mind."

"Don't you think I've tried? His mind is made up. He already paid and it's non-refundable; everything's settled. He's acting like he's doing me a big favour."

"What about your mom?"

"What about her? My dad bosses her around all the time. Just because he pays alimony he thinks he can run our lives. Besides, my mom's probably glad. In case you hadn't noticed, she's not exactly June Cleaver."

Actually, I hadn't noticed. Sure, Paul's mom seemed a little distracted ... well, maybe a little more than just distracted. Weird was a better way to describe her.

"Oh, Paul," I said, "this is the worst timing."

"It's not till the end of summer, and then we can always write."

"Yeah, sure," I said, "the story of my life."

"What?" Paul looked confused.

"Nothing," I said.

I felt nauseous, and watching thousands of ants scurry around behind the glass wasn't helping. In fact, I'd lost interest in all the bugs.

"Have you considered running away?" I asked.

"Where to?"

"My house. You could live in my basement! My parents never go down there."

"I think the phrase 'running away' refers to actually leaving the neighbourhood."

"That's the genius of it. No one would think to check my basement!"

"Clare, I appreciate your concern, but hiding out in your basement for a year doesn't really sound like much of a plan."

"Okay, you're right. So it won't be Plan A; it'll be Plan B. Give me some time; I'll work on a foolproof plan."

Paul looked doubtful.

We watched as a group of ants tried to organize themselves to transport what looked to me like a piece of dirt back to their nest. We just stood there, not saying anything.

"It's impossible," I finally said.

"Maybe not," said Paul. "Ants can lift six times their own body weight."

I glared at him. "I meant the prep school thing."

"Oh."

"Let's go, okay? I've had enough of these stupid bugs." I headed down the long darkened corridor toward the exit. Paul trailed behind me.

In the lobby of the museum, Paul showed me on a map where his new school was. It was clear across the country.

"Great," I said. "It may as well be on Mars."

"Clare, why are you acting like this is happening to you? I'm the one that has to leave. Do you have any idea what that's going to be like? I won't know anyone; I won't even know where to go to buy comic books or see a movie!" Paul looked defeated.

"Well it's just that you don't seem to be putting up much of a fight," I said.

"What am I supposed to do?" he asked, sighing.

"I don't know." I sighed, too. "You're right; I'm acting like a moron. I'm sorry."

We unlocked our bikes and rode toward our neighbourhood without talking. We stopped at the end of Paul's street and said goodbye. I couldn't think of one thing to say that would make him feel better. Mostly because I felt awful myself. When I got to my house, I put my bike in the garage and went in the back door to the kitchen. My mom was watching a cooking show on the little TV. She was chopping onions on a board and she smiled at me and kissed my forehead as I grabbed the phone out of its cradle and headed upstairs.

"Dinner's in twenty minutes, okay?" she said.

"Uh-huh," I said. I took the stairs two at a time and closed my bedroom door. I fell onto my bed and dialed Aunt Rusty's number. Her machine picked up.

"Hi. Rusty here. Can't come to the phone. If you're a friend or a relative, leave a name and number at the beep. Everyone else—go away."

I waited for the beep. I knew she might be there working.

"Aunt Rusty, it's me, Clare. Pick up if you're there. It's sort of an emergency." I waited a few seconds. Nothing. I hung up the phone. I looked down, and noticed that my foot was resting on my atlas, which was sticking out from under my bed. I hauled it out and opened it to the dog-eared Paris page. I looked at the red circle for a minute, then I got out a piece of paper and pen.

Dear Elsa,

I know this was all my idea and everything, but I really didn't think it through. I forgot that there would be moments when I would desperately need to talk to someone who wasn't my mom or Paul or Aunt Rusty. If you could just come back, that would be great. I'll do anything if you come back.

Please care,

Clare

P.S. We really should have worked out a code for emergencies.

Chapter 10

At school on Wednesday afternoon, something really strange happened. I was sitting in my usual place in Science class at the back of the classroom. I wasn't really paying attention (but really, does anyone after June first?) because I was going back and forth between feeling sorry for myself and thinking about how I could help get Paul out of his horrible situation. Let's face it, when you only have one friend, his situation is your situation. I wasn't coming up with anything even remotely practical. The best thing I'd thought of was that he could pretend he had a terrible life-threatening illness. The only downside would be that he would have to pretend to be sick for the whole summer and it would have to be a disease that was undetectable in a blood test. I didn't even know if such a disease existed. I made a note to myself to look up serious diseases on the internet and see if there were any that were undetectable in a blood test.

I was completely lost in thought when I suddenly felt a sharp stabbing sensation in the upper left side of my chest. My first thought, naturally, was that I was having a heart attack. My short, pathetic, unfulfilled life was over. I'd never been kissed, never been to a drive-in, never even driven a car! Before I jumped up and screamed for someone to dial 911, I thought about the heart attacks I'd seen on television. This didn't seem anything like that. I watched the clock until Science class was finally over; it was excruciating because I had to resist the urge to clutch my chest. When the buzzer finally went off, I walked calmly to the girls' bathroom. Thank God it was empty. I locked myself inside one of the flimsy turquoise cubicles and sat on the toilet lid. I lifted up my T-shirt and looked closely. Nothing. No gaping hole, no bone jutting through the skin, no bruises. I even felt around on my back for a bullet entry wound, to eliminate the possibility that I'd been shot without my knowledge (it happens!). I put my finger on my left nipple where the pain was coming from and I was shocked to discover a tiny lump, invisible to the naked eye, but definitely there. I could only conclude one thing: I was developing. At least, I *thought* I was developing. Maybe I was jumping the gun. If the lump somehow turned into a breast, I would look pretty weird with just the left one. Was this normal? Was it possible that breasts grow one at a time? I'd read somewhere that women's breasts are never both the same size. Who could I ask about this? Aunt Rusty. I remembered her telling me that day at the beach that she had developed overnight. I had no idea she could have meant that literally. What if I woke up tomorrow fully developed? I smiled at the thought of using the word "breasts" in reference to myself. Visions of plunging necklines and string bikinis rushed through my head. If only I could find Elsa and tell her I was developing.

I snuck past the vigilant hall monitor and arrived conspicuously late to Math class. I saw nothing and heard nothing. I felt hypnotized. I moved like a zombie for the rest of the day. When classes were finally over, I rode my bicycle home slowly, musing over the changes that were taking place in my body and how everything in the universe would change accordingly.

Again, I wished I could tell Elsa right away. Then I remembered how my last letter had been hysterical. I wanted to be level-headed about this. I wanted to prove that I could handle something big on my own. But could I? I also definitely didn't want my mom knowing. I had to be absolutely sure it wasn't some sort of twenty-four hour chest virus or a clogged pore or something. I hoped that whatever it was, it wouldn't affect my performance at the track meet, now only six days away. For the hundredth time I wondered why Elsa had come all the way from Paris to tell me I had to win that race. What did she have up her sleeve?

I took the phone into my room and called Aunt Rusty, but I got her machine again. I pressed redial over and over, but she never picked up. I didn't leave a message; this was not the kind of thing you left on someone's machine.

After dinner, when our asparagus risotto was digested, my mom and I went for a run. I was surprised to notice that "it" hurt when I ran. I wondered if this was a good sign. It was hard not to feel for it every few minutes just to make sure it was still there, like when you have a sore in your mouth and you keep touching it with your tongue.

I was relieved to get home from running so I could try to call Aunt Rusty again. This time she picked up the phone.

"Hey, where's the fire?" she said.

I told her that I'd explain about that later; something more important had come up. I described the pain in full detail.

"Yup, that's it all right," she said. "You're developing."

"Are you sure?" I asked. "Could it be something else?"

"No, I don't think so. Like what?"

"I don't know, a tumour, a virus, amoebic dysentery?"

"You're insane," she said. I heard the soft fizz of a diet-cola can opening. Aunt Rusty virtually lives on diet soda. I think she believes that the four major food groups are Diet Soda, Tootsie Rolls, Coffee and Gum.

"But the track meet is next Tuesday!" I said anxiously.

"And …?"

"Well, what if I can't run?"

"Can't run? Clare, you're not going to turn into Dolly Parton in six days!"

"Oh."

"You're going to be fine. You're just growing up. Isn't that what you always wanted?"

"I guess so."

"Listen, Clare, I gotta run, my paint's drying funny."

"Okay. Wait! Don't forget you promised you'd come to my track meet. You'll be there, right?"

"Wouldn't miss it for the world."

"Oh, and don't tell my mom about this, okay?"

"Of course not. But don't you think she'll figure it out?"

"I just don't want her to know yet."

"Clare?"

"Uh-huh?"

"Your mom's not the enemy. You know that, don't you?"

"Sure," I said. "Goodbye, Aunt Rusty."

I hung up the phone and put on my Spider-Man pajamas. I went to bed early without even talking to Paul, something I felt extremely guilty about. I just couldn't seem to focus on his problem. I'd stopped thinking about it right about the same time my body exploded into puberty. I tried to keep in mind that his problem was my problem, that my only friend on the planet was leaving. I tossed and turned and stared at the glow-in-the-dark stars on the ceiling of my bedroom for a long time before I finally fell asleep.

By Friday, the other side of my chest had started hurting, too, reassuring me that I wasn't some kind of freak, after all. I needn't have worried about my mom finding out, either. She already knew. Don't ask me how, though. I think moms have some sort of Spider-Sense when it comes to their kids.

My mom and I were running that night after supper; the hard part was behind us, and we'd reached the top of the excruciatingly steep hill that runs past the most beautiful houses in town, every one of them complete with a barking, drooling watchdog. We turned left at a sports field with two baseball diamonds and a soccer field, then headed into a wooded ravine. The early evening sun streamed through the trees and the cool, damp air smelled musky, like mould and mushrooms. I inhaled deeply. The rich air felt good in my tired lungs. I continued trying to talk my mom into buying me a new pair of sneakers.

"Really, Mom, these sneakers are pinching my toes."

"But they're brand new!" said my mom.

"Not really," I said. "I've had them almost six months, and my feet have probably grown a whole size since then. If my feet grow any faster, I'll have to wear clown shoes."

My mom laughed. It was a nice sound. I wondered why she didn't laugh more. "All right," she said, "but don't tell your dad, okay?"

"Don't worry, it's not like he'll even notice," I said sarcastically.

My mom ignored me. "Okay, we'll go shopping tomorrow and we'll get you a running bra, too. Now that you're developing, you shouldn't be running without some support."

I just about tripped over my great big feet. A running bra? For *me*? I was baffled. My mom may not win "Mom of the Year," but nothing got by her. I was officially developing now, and I was in the market for the proper equipment. After all, that's really what a running bra is, right? It's a piece of sports equipment like a tennis racket or a hockey stick.

"Okay," I said, "but it has to be black."

When we got back to the house, we both went for the fridge at the same time. I grabbed the water jug and poured us both a big glass. We heard my dad running on his treadmill in the den. I was going upstairs to change and shower when my dad called out to me. I stood in the doorway of the den.

"Hi, Dad," I said. He was going at quite a clip so it was hard for him to talk.

"Hi," *puff, puff.* "Where were you guys?" *Puff, puff.*

My mom came and stood in the doorway with me.

"Um, we were just out for a little run, that's all," I said.

"Yeah, that's all," said my mom. We exchanged glances.

"Hey," *puff, puff,* "next time you go," *puff, puff,* "let me know," *puff puff.* "I'll come along."

"Yeah, sure, Dad," I said.

"Yeah, that would be great," said my mom.

I started up the stairs and looked back at my mom. She looked at me and shook her head as if to say, "I won't tell him if you don't tell him."

I smiled at her and headed for the shower.

Dear Elsa,

I realize how distraught I must have sounded in my last letter, but it really did seem like the end of the world. Since then, something else has happened, so now I have good news and bad news. First, the good news:

I'm developing! It's not like I actually have breasts or anything, more like bumps really. I had no idea these things happened so fast, did you? It's like last week I was a kid and this week, BOOM! I'm a woman. I can't believe you're not here for this when we've been waiting and talking about it forever. My mom has been pretty cool about the whole thing. I wasn't expecting her to do back flips or anything, but she simply announced that we were going shopping for a running bra tomorrow. I'm getting a black one for two reasons: First of all, black is a very flattering colour on me, and second, Mr. Bianchini wears a black T-shirt almost every day, so I think black must be his favourite colour. Let me know if you're wearing any French lingerie yet, if you know what I mean.

Now for the bad news. Paul's dad is sending him to a private prep school in the East this fall. It's about a million miles away from here, so he'll only be home for major holidays. Just in case you're keeping score, that leaves me with zero friends. Who's going to notice my new breasts if I don't have any friends? Sure, it's true, Paul probably wouldn't notice them anyway, but who will I go out with so that other people will notice my new breasts? Sigh. As Scarlett O'Hara once said, "I won't think about it today; I'll think about it tomorrow. After all, tomorrow is another day."

More there,

Clare

Chapter 11

For everyone's information, running bras are kept in the lingerie department and not the sporting goods department as I had hoped. Needless to say, buying a running bra turned out to be a lot more traumatic than I thought it would be.

My mom and I found the lingerie department tucked away in a corner all on its own, and it was, in a word, pink. Pink everywhere you looked: walls, carpet, even the fitting rooms. A saleslady wearing pink floated over to us, smiling as though she were welcoming us into her own home.

"Good morning!" she said, clasping her hands together in front of her. "How can I help you today?" She flashed us a set of enormous teeth with fuchsia lipstick all over them. The better to eat me with, I'm sure. I contemplated making a run for it.

My mother took charge. She's always had a "take-no-prisoners" approach to shopping. "We're looking for running bras for my daughter," she announced.

"I see," said the saleslady, looking at my chest, or rather, looking *for* my chest. I swallowed hard.

"Have you ever been fitted for a bra, dear?" she asked me.

I opened my mouth but nothing came out. Finally I squeaked, "No."

My mother came to my rescue again. "I don't think that's necessary for a running bra, do you?"

I silently thanked her.

The pink saleslady seemed a little miffed. Measuring my measly chest seemed to be something she would have enjoyed immensely. It made me wonder what her days were like.

"All right then," she said curtly, "this way please." She ushered us to the proper section. She said, "Athletic bras come in extra-small, small, medium, large and extra large. We carry a wide variety of styles and colours." She showed us a blur of bras. She was well-versed in all aspects of the "athletic bra" but, looking at her, I had my doubts she'd ever worn one. One thing I knew for certain: this woman was born to sell lingerie.

Thankfully there was no one else in the department except a girl about my age and her mother. They appeared to be going through virtually the same process as we were and the girl looked as horrified as I felt. She caught my eye and made a face. We both laughed. She had long brown hair pulled into a ponytail, and she was wearing jeans with a tear in the knee exactly where my favourite jeans were torn. My mom wouldn't let me wear mine to the mall, though. I wanted to point out to her that these perfectly decent-looking people had no problem with torn jeans. The girl also had a fake tattoo of a butterfly on her right arm and she was chewing bright-green gum. I wondered why I'd never seen her before.

My mom chose about a hundred bras for me to try on and followed the saleslady to the pink fitting rooms. I reluctantly trailed behind. Soft music played as the lady unlocked the fitting room with a key from around her wrist. I personally questioned the need for high security. Why would anyone want to break into these stupid pink cubicles? Out, sure, but in?

My mom stood guard outside my fitting room as I danced in the mirror to a cheesy instrumental version of U2's "I Still Haven't Found What I'm Looking For" and tried on about half the bras she'd picked out. The other half were out of the question. I heard the girl with the brown ponytail talking to her mom about the bras she was trying on a few doors down. She was using words like "hideous" and "grotesque." It was kind of comforting.

My mom and I finally settled on two bras: a black one that I picked out and a flesh-toned one that my mom insisted on. Just whose flesh do they base the colour "flesh-tone" on, anyway? Certainly not mine. It reminded me of an Ace bandage, but my mom wasn't taking no for an answer, so I went along with it because she was such a good sport about the black one. The pink saleslady wrapped my bras in lots of pink tissue and put them in a shiny pink bag, which is the equivalent of carrying a neon sign that says, "I've been to the lingerie department!" She flashed her pink teeth at us one more time and wished us a pleasant day.

We headed out into the mall to the sporting goods store. After the bra-buying experience, buying sneakers was going to be a breeze. I was back in familiar territory. And I was right: my feet had grown another size. Maybe it was a fair trade-off for my new chest but I was ready for them to stop growing any time. I chose a pair of running shoes that were so comfortable I was pretty sure I could leap tall buildings in a single bound. I asked the gangly, pimply sales clerk in the referee's uniform for an extra-large bag so I could hide the pink lingerie bag inside it.

With both missions accomplished we headed back to the parking garage and searched for the car. In all the years we've been going places together, my mother and I have never once taken note of where the car is parked. Each level of the parking garage was conveniently named after a type of tree: Fir, Pine, Oak — basically the names of trees they cut down to build the mall. They all sounded the same to us. It would be so much easier if they named the levels after animals: Penguin, Grizzly Bear, Python. That I would remember. We finally found the car on Spruce, hiding between two suvs.

When we got home, I took the bags up to my room and unpacked the bras. I put the flesh-toned one in my drawer with my socks and I put the black one on. I posed in front of the mirror in it and tried it on with almost every piece of clothing in my closet, as though I would be wearing only the bra and nothing over it. I practised talking to Mr. Bianchini in my new bra for a while, then I took a pair of sweat socks and put one in each cup to get an idea of what I might look like down the road. I looked absurd. My mom came upstairs to tell me to wash the bras before I wore them. She walked in when I was one sock out and one sock in. At first she looked alarmed, but when she realized it was just a sock, she laughed.

"I actually went to school like that once," she said.

I tried to imagine my mom at my age, going to school with socks in her bra, but all I could picture was a girl in a little navy suit, carrying a briefcase, handing out business cards over lunch. It was impossible to imagine my mom ever being as lost as I feel sometimes.

It occurred to me that I hadn't thought about Paul all day. All this bra stuff had me completely preoccupied. I suddenly felt very selfish. His life was going down the toilet and I was dancing in front of my mirror like Madonna. I got the phone and dialed his number. He answered it on the first ring.

"Hello?"

"It's me," I said.

"Oh, hello."

"What are you doing?" I asked.

"Sorting, labelling and filing my microscope slides," he said.

"Hmmm, I don't suppose your dad's changed his mind or anything?"

"No. Now it looks like my mom wants me to go, too. I'm getting ambushed from both sides."

"What do you mean? Why does your mom want you to go?"

"I can't talk about it. They told me not to tell anyone."

"I'm not anyone. Tell me."

"No."

"Paul, I promise to keep it to myself or die."

Paul was quiet for a few seconds. "Okay. Meet me where the two seas part and the twin towers of agony cast no shadow." That's code for the Dairy Delite.

"When?" I asked.

"Four-and-a-half seconds."

"I'll be there," I said. We hung up without saying goodbye.

Chapter 12

A couple of hours later I left Paul at his corner and walked the rest of the way home alone. The late afternoon sun warmed the back of my neck and I walked slowly, digesting the root-beer float that was sloshing around in my stomach. I was also digesting everything Paul had just told me and thinking about how so many things had changed since the day I decided to say goodbye to Elsa. Maybe that's how it works; you take a leap and it sets everything in motion. I never realized that growing up could be so lonely. I always thought that it meant you would never be lonely again.

When I got home, my mom was still at the supermarket getting ingredients and my dad was still at the office (duh). I crawled out my bedroom window and sat on the roof hugging my knees and watching the horizon change from late-afternoon blue to early-evening orangey-pink. Saturdays would never be the same without Elsa. I started to shiver, and crawled back inside to write a letter.

Dear Elsa,

Things continue to happen at an alarming pace around here. Paul told me something he wasn't supposed to, so promise not to tell a soul what I'm about to tell you (especially not a Parisian. I've heard they love to talk).

Remember how Paul's mom always seemed a little odd? Remember how the drapes were always drawn in the middle of the day and she never seemed to go outside and she almost always had a cocktail glass in her hand? Well, it turns out she's an alcoholic. I guess sometimes you just get used to someone looking and acting a certain way and it never occurs to you that something's not right about it.

The reason Paul has to go to prep school so far away from here is that his mom is checking into an alcohol-treatment centre. And that isn't the worst of it. Paul has to spend the entire summer except for the first two weeks at his grandparents' house because that's when his mom's program starts. His grandparents live about four hundred miles away and Paul calls the place "Mr. Roger's Neighbourhood." But he says he'd rather stay there than with his dad and his dad's new girlfriend, Tamara. That's Paul's only other option. Apparently, Tamara is twenty-four and likes to wear a lot of spandex around the house and sometimes even (oh, horrors) out of the house. She calls herself a "Personal Trainer," but the only client she has is herself. Her nickname for Paul is "Little Einstein." You can see how that might become annoying.

Paul is really gloomy about all this. I feel so sorry for him. He knows that I want to help, but there really isn't anything I can do except listen. Parents can be the strangest people. You can live under the same roof with them and never really get to know them. Paul's situation really makes me appreciate my parents. I know they're not model parents or anything, but at least they aren't scary.

All this anxiety about Paul and the track meet (coming up on Tuesday!) has left me a basket case. I hope I can exhibit grace under pressure at the meet. I haven't been able to outrun Ginny since that time I told you about, but I somehow have a good feeling about this race. By the way, why is it suddenly so important to you that I win?

I almost forgot, I got a running bra (not a bra that runs, a bra you wear when you run). It's a black sports model. No one has noticed that I'm wearing it yet, but what was I expecting? People aren't going to be walking up to me saying, "Congratulations on the new breasts!" or anything like that. It makes me feel incredibly mature. It's amazing what a little piece of clothing can do. I haven't shown it to Aunt Rusty yet, but I can't wait to. I wish you could see it, too.

I was wondering about something today. I guess I always assumed that if you could claw your way out of childhood and into adulthood that the rest would be a breeze, but lately I've been wondering if that's true. Is it possible that adulthood is even tougher and lonelier than childhood? My mom said something to me today that made me wonder if she wasn't just as mixed up as me when she was a kid. Maybe she wasn't born a lawyer after all, and maybe she's scared of things now, too. Like being a mom, for instance. Let's face it, she was probably a better lawyer than she is a mother and all the other mothers already have loads of experience, so she's always playing catch-up. That has got to feel awfully lonely sometimes. And Paul's mom seems like the loneliest person in the world. How did she get that way?

No pressure, but I'm going to need some answers. So, if you could put down your croissant and stop flirting with French guys for a second, I'd appreciate you giving this some thought.

I'll write to you right after the track meet. Miss you.
Getting there,
Clare

Chapter 13

The morning of the track meet, I woke up early. A warm breeze drifted in through my open bedroom window, fluttering the sheer curtains. If it was already this warm, it would be sweltering by race time. I showered and dried my hair. One look in the mirror and it was clear that today was going to be a bad hair day. The humidity had sent my hair in all directions. I didn't let it bother me, though. I put on my new, freshly laundered bra and resisted the urge to wear a tight black tank top, which would have made things fairly obvious. Instead, I opted for the modest look of an oversized black T-shirt with King Kong on the front. It was probably the best I could do without my stylist. I laced up my sneakers and went downstairs.

My mom had an extra-large breakfast laid out on the kitchen table. An empty coffee cup and a newspaper sat at my dad's long-vacated spot. A home-cooked breakfast used to mean frozen toaster waffles, but today my mom had prepared freshly squeezed orange juice, whole-wheat pancakes with bananas on top and a bowl of granola. It was a breakfast of champions with about three weeks' worth of fibre. My mom can be very sensitive about her cooking, so I remembered to treat her with the same respect she had showed me when I was six and I'd presented her with my first culinary masterpiece baked under a light bulb in my Easy-Bake Oven.

"Mom," I said, "this looks delicious." I didn't have the heart to tell her that my stomach was in knots and I had absolutely no appetite.

"Thanks," she beamed, and sat down across from me with her coffee to watch me eat.

I focused on the fresh-cut daisies in the glass vase in front of me and choked down enough food to keep her happy. Every bite was a victory and I even remembered to say "Mmmm" from time to time. I put my dishes in the sink and kissed my mom goodbye. She said she'd see me at the finish line, clearly not understanding that I was about to run the most important race of my life.

I got my bike out of the garage, put my backpack on and started pedalling toward school. It was turning into one of those lazy summer days when all you want to do is jump into a cool swimming pool. I inhaled one hundred percent pure summer into my lungs. The knots in my stomach disappeared.

When I got to the school, things were already underway. There was a crowd gathered around the high-jump pit and the boys' relay was about to start. I went over to the sign-up table and a volunteer parent tried to give me a number "13" to pin on my T-shirt. I asked her if she was kidding me and she sighed and gave me number "66." The 800-metre relay was my first event. It was due to start in about fifteen minutes. I was dreading it because in practice all week my team had come in dead last. That was mostly because Keely Simon, our first runner, had a tendency to trip over her own feet.

I heard the announcement for my relay over the loud-speaker and headed over to the starting line. Keely wasn't even there yet, and I took that as a bad sign. She finally wandered over, looking very sleepy, seconds before the gun went off. Apparently, she isn't a morning person. Sure enough, the gun went off and Keely stumbled and fell about fifty feet into the race. I could hear my team groaning in unison all the way around the track. I managed to make up a lot of time on the last leg so that we weren't a complete disgrace, but we finished last anyway. Ginny Germain's team came in first. I just knew she was ticking off the events she would win in her head, starting with the relay. It made me want to win my event even more.

The day was becoming unbearably hot. Simply wandering around was becoming an effort, so I found a tree to sit under and stretched in the shade. Students were collapsing in piles in every square inch of available shade, and there were long lines at the water fountains. Ginny Germain sat under a tree chatting with a bunch of eighth-grade guys, oblivious to the fact that she should be getting ready for the race.

The loudspeaker announced my race, and everyone headed for the starting line. There were a lot of eighth-grade girls running the 800 metres because we're divided by age, not grade. I saw my mom in the crowd and waved to her, but I couldn't see Aunt Rusty yet. Mr. Bianchini was walking around with a clipboard, talking to parents, looking handsome. He was wearing a black T-shirt like mine. I automatically looked for Elsa before realizing she wasn't there. This was the first big race she wouldn't be watching.

The starter announced, "On your marks." I tried to shake the tension out of my limbs. I was already flushed from the heat and my heart was jumping around like a little rabbit. I hoped I wouldn't have a heart attack. How embarrassing it would be to drop dead at my seventh-grade track meet? And where was Aunt Rusty?

The gun went off and the herd shot forward. We immediately broke off into smaller packs. I was in the front pack. I could hear the pounding of sneakers around me and smell the churned-up grass and dirt as we stampeded around the field. My heart seemed to be beating inside my head and it felt as though it would explode. I was neck-and-neck with four girls at the front of the pack; three of them were eighth graders and one of them was Ginny Germain.

As we headed into the second lap, I finally saw Aunt Rusty holding a colourful Japanese paper umbrella over her head and jumping up and down. She was screaming, "Go Clare, c'mon girl, RUN!" She was creating quite a spectacle. I smiled to myself. Ginny and I ran together for most of the second lap, but I finally dug deep inside myself and managed to find a tiny bit of extra power. I turned it on. My body slipped into a higher gear and edged ahead of Ginny. It was a scene right out of a movie. I flew over the finish line inches ahead of her. I'd won! And this time it really meant something!

I wandered around, gasping for air. The heat caught up to me and I felt dizzy, so I bent over, trying to catch my breath. When I straightened up, Aunt Rusty and my mom were both there. They both hugged me at once. I was deliriously happy. I scanned the crowd for Mr. Bianchini and I finally saw the back of his head. He was tending to one of the racers who'd fainted after the race; she probably hadn't eaten breakfast. Mr. Bianchini turned around and looked right at me. He smiled and gave me a thumbs up. Then his gaze drifted elsewhere. I tried to see who or what he was looking at. Then I figured it out. She was wearing a short little skirt and black lace-up army boots. Her long red hair was pulled back into a ponytail. Mr. Bianchini was looking at Aunt Rusty and I didn't like what I saw in his eyes.

All of a sudden, everything seemed to move in slow motion. Mr. Bianchini came over and congratulated me. My mom introduced him to Aunt Rusty. They shook hands and smiled at each other like they shared some sort of secret. It was disgusting. I thought to myself, *Hey, wait a minute, isn't this supposed to be about ME? Let's talk about ME some more! Did you see that race? Did anyone see that race?*

A volunteer parent holding a clipboard came over and handed me a first-place ribbon. I muttered, "Thanks," and snatched the ribbon out of her hand. She looked surprised; I don't suppose many first place winners behave that way.

We were allowed to leave the track meet when our events were finished, and my mom suggested we go for ice cream. I was happy to leave. The mid-day heat had taken its toll on everyone; students were dropping like flies.

"Aunt Rusty," I said, "we're going for ice cream now." I looked at her pleadingly. She ignored me. She was listening to something clever Mr. Bianchini was saying.

"Aunt Rusty!" I raised my voice and tugged on the sleeve of her T-shirt. "Time to go for ice cream!" I could hear my voice becoming shrill. She finally shifted her attention to me. She was smiling.

"Oh, I can't. I gotta get back to my studio."

"You're an artist?" asked Mr. Bianchini.

I mumbled goodbye and Aunt Rusty waved at us half-heartedly as she started to tell Mr. Bianchini about her life's work.

My mom and I walked off the field. I kept looking back over my shoulder to see if Aunt Rusty and Mr. Bianchini were still talking. They were becoming more animated and laughing a lot. I wanted to know what they were saying. What could they possibly have in common? They're not at all alike. Aunt Rusty is practically a vampire and Mr. Bianchini is a healthy, fit, active, outdoorsy type. Besides, I saw him first!

I sat across from my mom in a booth at the Dairy Delite and sipped my root-beer float without even tasting it. I tapped my fingers impatiently on the Formica table top, wondering what had happened at the school after we left. I prayed Mr. Bianchini was just being polite to Aunt Rusty. My mom was clearly oblivious to what I was feeling. She kept telling me how proud she was of me. I thought: *Blah, blah, blah, it's just a stupid race. Who cares about a stupid race? Can't you see what's really going on? Aunt Rusty's stealing my boyfriend!*

Chapter 14

Dear Elsa,

Well, I hope you're happy. I won the stupid race. I don't really have much time to write; I'm busy blacking out photos of Mr. Bianchini in my yearbook with a magic marker. After that, I'm going to cut Aunt Rusty's head out of every picture I have of her. Are you ready for this? Aunt Rusty and Mr. Bianchini are dating! (She calls him Len. Ugh, I could die. My new name for him is "Bink the Fink.") They met at MY track meet, to which I invited Aunt Rusty, so I get the added agony of blaming myself.

Here's what keeps going through my head: a wedding. I'm the bridesmaid, Aunt Rusty's the bride and she's all in black. She's walking down the aisle to marry the man I've dreamed about for all of my formative years, and suddenly he's my Uncle Lenny. It could happen! I was such a fool to think that a running bra or a black T-shirt or winning a race could actually make a difference. I am so stupid!

Maybe I should have told Aunt Rusty how I felt about Mr. Bianchini, but I could never say it out loud, and besides, who could have predicted this disaster? The only good thing about winning the race is that now I compete at the district finals next week against all the other schools in the area. I vow to win this race without the help of Mr. Bianchini. After all, it doesn't take a genius to work a stopwatch. After the district track meet, school's out for the summer and I don't have to think about this mess until September. "Bink the Fink" teaches eighth-grade P.E., too, so I'm going to ask my mom if I can change schools.

I have to go. My mom is waiting for me to go running with her. It used to be fun, but now it's serious. Now I have something to prove.

Beware,

Clare

The heat wave was still making the days pretty unbearable, but in the early evening a soft breeze came up just in time for my run with my mom. We still came home each night drenched in sweat, though.

My mom, thankfully, didn't mention you-know-who and you-know-who-else's new "relationship" on our run. Instead, she focused on her latest preoccupation: my birthday, which was coming up in three weeks. I'm grateful that my birthday falls after school is out for the summer so I don't have the pressure of planning a party that no one would come to. I guess I never really had to worry about it too much, though, since my mom's always been too busy in the past to plan much. She asked me what I wanted this year.

"A pony," I answered without hesitation.

"No, really, Clare."

"Okay, a dog," I said. "I really want a dog." I figured it was worth another try. This is part of my birthday ritual. Every year my parents ask me what I want and every year I say "a dog," and then they go out and get me what they think I need.

My mom sighed. "Clare, every year I ask you what you want for your birthday and every year you say 'a dog.' We've been through this a thousand times. Your dad doesn't want a dog."

"I know he doesn't," I said. "I do. He has his own birthday."

"Well, unfortunately he pays the mortgage, and he says dogs are too much work."

"What does he care? He won't be doing any of it."

"Well, he says they tear up the yard," she said, wiping sweat off her forehead with the palm of her hand.

"Dad never even uses the yard. When was the last time he was even *in* the yard?"

"That's not the point. I'm sorry, Clare, I really am, but you can't have a dog. Isn't there anything else you want, anything at all?"

"No," I answered coldly.

"Well then, I guess I'll just have to surprise you."

We came to the steep hill and we were both quiet for the gruelling climb. I was thankful for the hill because I was finished talking. I hadn't actually thought my mom would agree to getting a dog, but I liked adding her refusal to the ever-growing list of things that had gone wrong in my life lately. I had naively thought that the second I started to develop, everything would change for the better. But it hadn't worked out like that at all. In fact, the opposite had happened.

When I got home, I pulled off my sweaty running clothes and left them in a smelly heap on the floor. It was still pretty early in the evening, so I changed into my cutoff jeans and a T-shirt and went out the back door. As the screen door slammed behind me, I heard the phone ring and my mom telling Aunt Rusty I was out. I stood below the kitchen window and listened, but all I heard was a lot of "I don't know" and "Uh-huh." I got on my bike and rode over to Paul's.

Things at Paul's house were pretty gloomy, so I let him choose what we would do. That always means Scrabble. We lay on the carpet in Paul's basement, the coolest room in the house. I crunched a cheese doodle as I contemplated my crappy set of letters. I finally put down "LAKE" for a measly sixteen points. Paul put down the word "FAQIR" for forty-six points. It looked awfully suspicious to me.

"What," I asked, "is a faqir?"

"It's an Indian snake charmer," he said.

"Yeah, sure," I said. "You made it up; I'm challenging."

"Be my guest," he said smugly, pointing to the Scrabble dictionary. "But bear in mind what happened the last nine times you challenged me."

"Ah, forget it," I said. "You can keep your stinking faqir." I didn't feel like being humiliated by Paul again. I had only agreed to play because I was trying to make him feel better, anyway.

Paul won, as usual, and I refused to play another game. I really wished I could talk to someone about Aunt Rusty, but I knew I couldn't talk to Paul. He's always disliked her. I didn't want to hear "I told you so" from him. So after an hour or so at his house, I made up a lame excuse about having homework to do and I rode my bike home.

It was still hot in the house, and my mom was making lemonade. She handed me a glass as I passed her on my way up to my room. I heard her turn on some music and I wondered again if she felt lonely sometimes. I'm sure this wasn't what she'd pictured when she decided to stop being a lawyer. Did she think I'd be standing there waiting to be her best friend in the whole world? What about the other twelve years of my life? If it hadn't been for Elsa, I don't know what I would have done.

I put on the Marilyn Monroe T-shirt that I wear as a nightshirt and climbed out my bedroom window with my lemonade to sit on the roof. The sun was slowly sliding out of the sky. Everyone in the neighbourhood sat on their porches in swings and rockers that sat empty most of the rest of the year. Hot summer nights can be sort of magical.

I hugged my knees to my chest and thought about my upcoming summer, which was looking pretty bleak. School was finished in a week, Paul was gone in less than two weeks and Aunt Rusty was completely out of the picture. What was I going to do with my summer? I'd been toying with the idea of signing up for a track-and-field summer camp I'd seen advertised on the bulletin board at school, but I had to be absolutely sure that Mr. Bianchini wasn't one of the instructors.

Every time I thought about Mr. Bianchini and Aunt Rusty, I felt a pain in my chest — actual, physical pain. Could this be what a broken heart feels like? Was it possible that Mr. Bianchini had actually broken my heart? I sighed. I gave that man the best years of my life, and all I got was chest pain.

I suddenly got the feeling that I wasn't alone on the roof. Then I saw Elsa's tan slender legs next to mine. She was wearing Moroccan leather sandals and a pretty blue sleeveless dress with flowers on it. I looked over at her and smiled. She was fanning herself with a slender black book.

"My gosh, I don't remember it ever being so hot around here," she said.

"What brings you back?" I asked.

"Well, I was getting all these letters: 'come home,' 'don't come home'; some really mixed messages. And then this thing about Aunt Rusty! Is it true?"

I nodded.

"That traitor! Have you spoken to her?"

"Nope," I said. "She calls, but I won't talk to her. I can't imagine what I'm supposed to say to her. 'Oh, by the way Aunt Rusty, your new boyfriend is the love of my life, so could you please break up with him immediately?'"

"Would you like to put a curse on her? I've learned a thing or two abroad. In fact, I spent a weekend in Algiers and …"

"That's okay; I think my days of putting curses on people are over."

"Really?" Elsa looked annoyed. "Well then, we'll have to do it the old-fashioned way and just wait it out, I guess. Does Mr. Bianchini know she's a witch?"

"She's not a witch," I said.

"Okay, maybe not, but you couldn't exactly call her wholesome, could you? Wasn't her last boyfriend Boris Karloff? Trust me, it won't last."

I laughed. "Oh Elsa, I miss you so much."

Elsa looked wistful. "Me, too," she said. "Oh, before I forget, bravo on the race! Now you just have to win the district finals, okay?"

"I'll try my best, but what if I don't?"

"Just do." Elsa looked at her naked wrist. "Yikes, is that the right time? I've got to run; I'm going to a summer solstice party in Cairo. We'll be dancing and eating all night long."

"Who's we?"

Elsa shrugged. "Me and some friends."

"Some friends? What do these friends do?" I asked, mom-style.

"A little of this, a little of that," she said mysteriously.

Suddenly, I was alone on the roof again. The moon was out now and the sky was starting to fill with stars.

I looked at the place where Elsa had been sitting. The book she'd been fanning herself with was still there. It was black and looked very old. I picked it up and looked at it. The leather cover was cracked and stained. It said "*The Prophet* by Kahlil Gibran" in gold letters. A page was marked with a little piece of paper. I opened the book to the yellowing page and read:

> "*When your friend speaks his mind you fear not the 'nay'*
> *in your own mind, nor do you withhold the 'ay.'*
>
> *And when he is silent your heart ceases not to listen*
> *to his heart;*
>
> *For without words, in friendship, all thought, all desires,*
>
> *all expectations are born and shared, with joy*
> *that is unacclaimed.*
>
> *When you part from your friend, you grieve not;*
>
> *For that which you love most in him may be*
> *clearer in his absence,*
>
> *as the mountain to the climber is clearer from the plain.*"

I closed the book and held it up to my face and smelled French perfume and musky oldness. Then I climbed back inside and slipped it under my bed on top of the atlas.

Chapter 15

The morning of the district track meet I slept late. For some strange reason, my mother, who usually wakes me promptly at seven, forgot. I was having a bizarre dream about a man chasing me on a motorcycle. He was wearing black leather and a black helmet with dark sunglasses. I was barely managing to stay ahead of him. There were people standing on both sides of the street cheering me on, and among them I recognized a few of my neighbours. I realized I was running up my own street. I passed my house and my mom was standing on the porch waving at me. I looked over my shoulder. The guy was inches away from me. He was smiling maniacally. There was something strangely familiar about his face. Thankfully, I woke up just as his front tire touched the back of my thigh. I could still hear the sound of the motorcycle, but it seemed to be coming from the kitchen. I sat up and looked at my alarm clock. It was a quarter to eight. I jumped out of bed and ran downstairs.

My mom shut off the blender when she saw me and poured its green contents into a glass.

"Mom, it's almost eight!" I said. "Why didn't you wake me?"

She glanced up at the clock over the doorway. "It's seven forty-five. You've got plenty of time. Here, drink this." She handed me a glass of green stuff.

I took a sip and made a face. "Did you forget that today is my track meet?"

"Of course not," she said, adding a handful of strawberries to the concoction in the blender. A strand of brown hair fell across her face and she tucked it behind her ear. I'd noticed lately that my mom made fewer trips to the beauty salon; she no longer looked like a TV anchorwoman. She rarely wore makeup and she somehow seemed softer and more feminine, even though she wore jeans most of the time.

"I'll drive you, okay?" she asked.

I nodded.

"How's the drink?" she asked.

"What is it?"

"A power drink. I've been juicing all morning."

"Why is it green?"

"Spirulina. It cleanses your blood."

"Yum." I handed the glass back to her. "I'm going up to take a shower."

I heard the blender going again as I got into the shower. Who did she think was going to drink all that stuff? The juicer and the blender were the latest in my mother's new obsession with small appliances. They would soon start collecting dust in the small appliance parade that was marching down the countertop and included the pasta maker, the waffle iron and the bread maker. The people who'd given her the espresso machine had created a monster. Our kitchen was starting to look like my mom was a contestant on *The Price Is Right*.

The district track meet was being held at a school across town from my school. My mom listened to a classic rock-and-roll radio station on the way there and sang along to "Imagine" by John Lennon. I hate it when I'm anxious and other people are calm. We got there with plenty of time to spare.

Even though the school really isn't that far from mine, it felt like a foreign country. Other schools always seem so intimidating to me. My mom dropped me off out front and went to park the car and, I suspected, to meet Aunt Rusty, but she wasn't talking. I'd overheard enough of my mom's phone conversations to know that Aunt Rusty was going to be at the meet. I didn't care. In fact, I was glad; it would make my victory even sweeter.

The sports field was huge and full of strangers. I made my way to the sign-in table, read the posted schedule of events and found my race. It didn't start for half an hour. I signed in and a perky mom handed me a number "43" to pin on the white school-issued T-shirt we were forced to wear so you could tell the schools apart. I found a place on the sidelines to sit on the grass and watch some events. The girls' hurdles for my age group were about to start, and I recognized a couple of girls from my school in the line-up. There was also a girl I'd seen somewhere before who didn't go to my school. Her long brown ponytail looked familiar. I kept my eye on her as the gun went off and she took off like an eager racehorse. She sailed over the first hurdle well ahead of the other runners. I watched in awe as she cleared each hurdle without losing her pace at all. She made it seem effortless. The rest of the hurdlers fell way behind her and she won the race easily. When it was over, I realized I'd been holding my breath — I'd really wanted her to win. I saw her in the crowd at the end of the race. No one came over to congratulate her. She just stood there alone, catching her breath. I stood up and went to look for an empty spot on the grass to stretch and prepare for my race.

A few minutes later, they announced my race over the loudspeaker and I headed to the starting line. The track was a deluxe model compared to the one at my school. It made ours look like a cow path. It was made of crushed red rock with crisp, freshly painted white lines. They must have held a heck of a bake sale to afford this.

Since this was the finals, there was only a small group of girls running: first, second, and third fastest from each school. I saw Ginny Germain and said hello. She said hello back with exactly the same amount of enthusiasm. Four girls down on my right was the girl with the brown ponytail. Suddenly I was very nervous. I tried to think of all the good things about running here today. First, it was much cooler than it had been the day of my school's track meet. There were puffy white clouds forming in the sky, blocking out the sun; ideal running weather. Second, the track was much faster; if I could do well on our school's cow path of a track, I could do even better here.

I caught sight of my mom on the sidelines and waved to her. She was standing next to a man in a suit talking on a cell phone. I thought he looked ridiculous until I realized it was my dad!

The gun went off, taking me by surprise. I shot forward. These girls weren't fooling around. We set a pace and ran in a tight pack, inches away from each other for the entire first lap. At the beginning of the second lap, I nosed ahead of the pack. I felt powerful; no one wanted to win this race as much as I did. I sprinted with everything I had and, miraculously, the pack slowly fell behind me. I was running alone. All I could hear was my own breathing. The crowd seemed to disappear.

About halfway into the second lap, I heard someone coming up on my right. Ginny Germain? No. Out of the corner of my eye I saw a brown ponytail bobbing up and down. She was gaining on me fast. Suddenly the ponytail was right in front of me. She had a fake tattoo of a butterfly on her arm. It finally dawned on me. I knew who she was. The lingerie department. It was the girl from the lingerie department and she was sailing past me to win *my* race!

Dear Elsa,

Let's just get it out of the way. I came in second at the district track meet. It was a little disappointing, since I only wanted to win more than anything in the world and also because you-know-who and you know-who-else were both there watching. My mom told me I should be grateful for Aunt Rusty's support. Ha! If my aunt were so supportive, she wouldn't have snatched my boyfriend away! (Okay, maybe she doesn't know she snatched my boyfriend away.)

I guess coming in second is acceptable, considering I was running against the best in the district, including a lot of eighth graders (who ate my dust, by the way).

Here's the weird part, though. The girl who beat me is a girl I saw in the lingerie department the day I went to get my running bra (believe me, every detail of that day is etched forever in my memory). And then she turns up out of nowhere to beat me in a race. After the race, she came right over to me and said, "Wow, that was close. Great race." All I could think of to say was, "Yeah, you, too." Brilliant, Clare. Then I lost sight of her as she disappeared into the crowd.

You won't believe who else was at the race: my dad! He actually turned off his cell phone to watch me finish; well, at least he said he did. I don't think my dad's ever seen me run before. I didn't even think he knew I ran. I was happy to see him, and grateful too, because having my dad there meant I didn't have to talk to Aunt Rusty, who came bouncing over in some sort of floral sundress (I'm not kidding, floral!). She tried to trick me into talking to her, but I played it really cool. I couldn't help but notice that she actually had a little colour in her cheeks, and this part you won't believe: she was eating a banana! Remember when her idea of fruit was cherry-flavoured gum?

Aunt Rusty didn't seem put off by my coolness at all. Mr. Bianchini came over and they started telling my mom a story. Something about Aunt Rusty's attempt at cooking fish. I strained to hear what they were saying and tried to concentrate on what my dad was talking about at the same time. Aunt Rusty was laughing and Mr. Bianchini was looking more handsome than ever. He was beaming at her. I was filled with rage for both of them.

I've decided to enroll in track-and-field camp in an attempt to enhance my upcoming summer. It starts the second week of July. I called the number on the brochure I got from the bulletin board at school and asked, in a cleverly disguised voice, who the instructors would be. The woman on the phone read the list to me. Mr. Bianchini wasn't on it. Just to make sure, I said, "What about Mr. Bianchini? I hear he's very good." She said, "Oh yes, he's wonderful, but he's decided to take the summer off this year." Then she said, "Between you and me, I think he's in love." Then she chuckled like that was funny or something. My chest started hurting. I thanked her and hung up.

Well, I guess that's about it. Good, bad, and worse. School is over tomorrow. Thank God. I'm exhausted.

Still there,

Clare

Chapter 16

The first day of summer vacation I purposely slept late. I finally woke up to the sweet sound of birds chirping in the oak tree outside my open window. They seemed to be saying "You're free! You're free!" The first day of summer vacation is the sweetest day of the year. You have a whole summer full of possibility stretched out endlessly ahead of you. I yawned and stretched luxuriously.

The day before had been a frenzy of textbook returns ("No, really, I swear it looked just like that when I got it last September") and the ritualistic emptying of lockers. Large plastic garbage cans lining the hallways overflowed with the debris that no one wanted to take to the next grade; a dumpster in each hallway would have been more practical. My locker was no exception. I found some petrified fruit, an unidentifiable science experiment (at least I think that's what it was), a bicycle tire tube, a pump, a pair of sandals I thought I'd lost and $2.46 in loose change. I pocketed the change, put the sandals on and put the pump, the tube and my shoes in my backpack. I happily threw everything else away. I moved on to my gym locker, where I found some very smelly gym clothes, which I stuffed into my backpack. Under the gym clothes, I found a picture of Mr. Bianchini I'd cut out of the school newspaper months ago. He was talking to a group of students, squinting in the sun. I looked at it for a minute, then I crumpled it up and threw it in the trash.

Students were running up and down the hallways, whooping and hollering, signing yearbooks and saying their goodbyes. I exited through the front doors of the school for the last time as a seventh grader. As I walked around the back of the school to the bike rack, I quietly said a grateful goodbye to seventh grade and all the suffering that went with it, bearing in mind that I hadn't officially passed into eighth grade until I got my report card in the mail.

All that was behind me now; summer had officially begun and I could be anyone I wanted. I lingered in bed for a few minutes then forced myself to get up. I looked out the window. The sky was a brilliant blue and it was the perfect temperature — not too hot, not too cold. My mom's car wasn't in the driveway, but I heard somebody rummaging around the kitchen. I found a T-shirt and shorts on the floor and pulled them on and, just to be on the safe side, I grabbed an old tennis racket out of the closet in case there was an intruder down there trying to steal our mayonnaise. I crept down the stairs, avoiding the creaks, and turned the corner into the kitchen to find Paul's rear-end sticking out of the refrigerator.

"Paul?" I said, lowering the tennis racket.

He jumped, banging his head on the inside of the fridge.

"Oh, hi," he said, rubbing the back of his head. He held

up a loaf of banana bread wrapped in cellophane. "Can I eat this?"

"Sure," I said. "Make yourself at home."

Paul noticed the racket. "You play tennis?" he said.

"No." I put the racket down. "Paul, why are you in my kitchen?"

"Your mom told me to wait for you." Paul pulled out a chair and sat at the table. He unwrapped the banana bread and smelled it for signs of spoilage.

"She baked it yesterday," I said, pulling a large knife out of the drawer to stick in his throat. I thought better of it, and placed it next to him.

"Oh," said Paul. He picked up the knife and lopped off a large slice. He held it in mid-air until I handed him a plate from the cupboard. "Thanks," he said.

"Where is she?" I asked.

"Who?"

"My mom."

"Oh. She went to the supermarket." Paul took a large bite of banana bread. "Do you have any milk?" he asked with his mouth full.

I opened the fridge and took out a carton of milk. I took a glass from the cupboard and filled it.

"Wait a minute," said Paul. "What's the expiration date on that?"

I looked at the top of the carton. "It's not for a week," I answered impatiently.

"What year?"

"Do you want it or not?" I slammed the glass down in front of him.

Paul smelled the milk and took a few tentative sips followed by another large bite of banana bread.

"Did we have plans for today?" I asked, running my fingers through my hair.

Paul motioned for me to wait while he chewed and swallowed. "Nothing specific," he said, "but I have a few ideas I'd like to run by you."

"Like what?" I said, leaning against the counter. I wasn't sure I wanted to know. If he said Scrabble I was throwing him out.

"Well, I thought we'd start out at a garage sale down at the end of Birch Street. I saw it advertised in the newspaper and it says they have comic books; of course, I called several times to confirm. After that, I thought we might head down to the miniature golf course and play a couple of rounds, that is, weather permitting, of course."

I looked out the kitchen window. "There's not a cloud in the sky!"

"I watched the weather channel and there's a ten percent chance of a shower this afternoon."

I sighed. "Okay, why not? Give me five minutes. I'll go get ready."

"Don't forget to pack a rain jacket. Better safe than sorry."

I was already on my way up the stairs. "Thanks, but I'll take my chances. I'm feeling lucky."

"Oh, I almost forgot!" he yelled after me. "Your mom told me to tell you she's having a barbecue tonight."

"Thanks," I yelled back sarcastically.

"... and she invited me for dinner!"

I slammed the bathroom door.

At first I was annoyed with Paul for planning the entire first day of my summer vacation, but I ended up having a really good time. At the garage sale I found a worn-in base-ball cap for twenty-five cents and a book on the care and training of Labradors for fifty cents. Paul got a whole stack of comic books for a dollar because he put a ratty old *Archie* on top of the pile and tried to look pathetic. The woman was happy to take the money. What she didn't know was that there were two valuable Spider-Man comics in the stack. Of course Paul knew exactly what they were worth. He has all that stuff memorized. He's one of those collec-tors who orders special bags to put his valuable comic books in and special boxes to put the bags in. I'm one of those collectors who usually eats a Hershey bar while reading my latest acquisition. My comic books are all carefully stored in a heap somewhere on the floor of my bedroom.

We rode our bikes about five miles to the north side of town to the miniature golf course and played three rounds. I won all three rounds because Paul analyzes every shot like he's on the pro tour or something and then he blows it anyway. The loser had to buy the winner an ice cream. I got two scoops of mint chip and Paul got vanilla because he's Paul.

After we finished our ice cream we went on the bumper cars until Paul got a headache from me slamming into him. By that time we were out of money anyway, so we rode our bikes to my house and read comic books in the shade of the oak tree in my backyard. My mom barbecued burgers and my dad shocked us all by making it home in time for dinner. He also surprised us by knowing Paul's name without being prompted. It never did rain; in fact, it was the perfect summer day.

After he had eaten everything there was to eat, including three helpings of berry crumble, Paul finally left. I was cleaning up the kitchen with my mom when the phone started ringing. My mom quickly plunged both hands in dishwater to trick me into answering it. I stared at it as it kept ringing.

"You better get that, it could be work for your dad," she lied.

I finally grabbed it. "Hello?"

"Clare, it's Aunt Rusty."

There was no escaping; she had me. I glared at my mom, who was watching, pretending not to.

"Hullo," I said cautiously.

"I was just looking at today's list of things to do and I noticed that number two is *Make things right with Clare*, right after *Buy Diet Coke* and right before *Do laundry*. So, how about it?"

"How about what?" I went into the living room, out of my mom's earshot, and flopped onto the sofa. I couldn't have annoyed my mother more, I'm sure.

"How about you tell me what's going on?"

"What do you mean?"

"I mean, why are you so upset that I'm dating Len?"

Len, ugh! Didn't she know that hearing that name was torture?

"I'm not."

"Are you sure?"

"Well, if I was, would you break up with him?"

"No, Clare, I wouldn't."

"So you care more about Mr. Bianchini than you care about me?"

"Am I really supposed to choose between you? Isn't that just a little … oh, I don't know … INSANE?!"

"Would you like some time to think about it?" I asked calmly.

"No, but I'd like you to take a little time to think about how unreasonably you're behaving."

Ouch! Aunt Rusty sounded like my mom.

"Okay, I will!"

"Okay, then."

"Goodbye!"

"Goodbye." I wanted to slam the phone down, but they don't make phones like that anymore, so I pressed the END button very aggressively.

Chapter 17

Dear Elsa,

It's official. My report card danced into the mailbox this morning; I'm done with seventh grade. Good riddance, I say! I will never have to deal with seventh-grade problems again. I have exactly eight-and-a-half weeks to reinvent myself and emerge an eighth grader. It's all going to be different now. I think.

Paul has become a black hole of emotional need. I actually had to tell him I was sick so I could escape and write this letter. He told me it was probably that hot dog I ate at the baseball game (YES! We went to a baseball game) and I should call him the minute I'm feeling better. I know what he's doing. He's trying to fit a whole summer's worth of fun into thirteen days because he knows it's really going to suck after that.

Every morning for the past five mornings the doorbell has rung promptly at nine, and it was Paul, with the agenda for the day. Even my mom's getting sick of him. Suddenly she has all these important things to do right around nine. She's probably parked around the corner with binoculars watching till the coast is clear so she can come home.

So far we've been to the zoo (twice), the art museum, the aquarium, the miniature golf course, three movies, and we even went to the waterslides! I know what you're thinking: Paul at the waterslides? It was pretty hard not

to laugh when he walked out of the men's locker room in his
baggy plaid swim trunks with his skinny white legs. He sort
of looked like he was riding a chicken. He lost his glasses
at the bottom of the pool and I had to dive down for them
about fifty times before I found them because people kept
flying off the end of the slide, churning up the water and I
couldn't see a thing down there.

The next day we went hiking down the trails that
follow the reservoir. Paul twisted his ankle while
consulting the trail map for the billionth time. I had to
find him a stick to lean on. It was either that or carry
him. He hobbled all the way home and the trip ended up
taking four times as long as it should have. The next day
his ankle was miraculously healed.

One of the wonderful things I've noticed about summer
is that all the stupid school rules don't apply. You can go
anywhere you want and no one knows who you are, what
grade you're in or how popular you are. Summer vacation
is the great equalizer. (If anyone asks, I tell them Paul
is my older, adopted brother.)

In other news, I'm noticing strange and wonderful
developments in the development department. Sometimes
I think I'm just imagining it, but the other day at the
waterslides I was premiering my first bikini ever (buying
a bikini is an entirely different experience from buying
a bra. They actually leave you completely alone, who
knew?), and I swear a couple of boys looked twice at me.
They were probably total jerks, but at least I know I'm

not invisible to members of the opposite sex. Of course, I went home and spent hours locked in the bathroom, looking at myself from the side in the mirror. There's no question about it; I'm growing.

I've also decided to grow my hair over the summer. It's part of a new image I'm planning for the fall, since my mom won't let me change schools. It's almost long enough to squeeze into a ponytail, especially if I use about 75 bobby pins.

I still haven't been able to bring myself to forgive Aunt Rusty. My mom told me she quit smoking. Yeah, right. Quitting smoking for Aunt Rusty would be like quitting breathing. I'm sure she sneaks cigarettes when Mr. Bianchini's not around. Maybe she can fool him, but she can't fool me. The thought of those two together still makes me nauseous.

I've been thinking I should get Paul a going-away present, but after spending every waking moment with him for the past week, I'm not feeling all that charitable. I feel more like getting him a "Glad-you're-going-away" present. I thought I might buy him a book on paleontology, or biology, or removing your own appendix or something like that. I suppose I have a lot to be grateful for. I was dreading an empty summer and so far I haven't had one moment to myself.

My mom, in another attempt to bond with me, has asked me to take part in a 5K Mother-Daughter Run for Breast Cancer. It's this Saturday. At first I wanted to tell her no. I hate that "Mother-Daughter, We're-a-Team" stuff, but then I thought, it's for a good cause and it might be fun. I told her I would do it. We don't have a lot of time to get pledges, but we talked my dad into a big pledge.

I guess I'd better go. I have a lot to do before Paul finds out I'm faking sick.

More or less there,

Clare

Chapter 18

A giant pink caterpillar of mothers and daughters wearing matching pink BREAST CANCER AWARENESS T-shirts ran, walked, and bladed in a parade that snaked for about a half a mile through town. Women of all ages, races, and sizes were there, and I was one of them. I looked over at my mom and smiled. I was getting that warm, fuzzy feeling you get when you know you're part of something important. My mom told me in the car that there would be a lot of cancer survivors in the race, women who had lost part or all of a breast or even both of their breasts. I was surprised at how joyful all these women seemed. Everyone was laughing and talking and making friends. I thought about all the time I'd wasted worrying about when I would finally develop. Maybe having breasts isn't so important after all. To some of these women, being alive and healthy was enough.

The race was a breeze. It was fun to run for a cause instead of for myself. I liked the fact that I didn't have to compete. All I had to do was finish. The race ended at a park in a valley. A stage was set up and volunteers served lemonade and cookies. It took a while for all of the women to come in. It was great to see the looks on their faces as they finished the race; they all looked so victorious. Some of the mothers were in wheelchairs being pushed by their daughters and some of the daughters were in strollers being pushed by their mothers.

My mom and I sat on the grass with our lemonades and talked with some of the other women. My mom found another ex-lawyer and latched onto her. They had a lot to talk about. I watched my mom's face and I realized that she wasn't the same person she had been when she was a lawyer. She smiled more often, and the worry lines on her forehead weren't so prominent. She seemed more peaceful.

When most of the women had finished the race, the head of the local Breast Cancer Foundation got up on the stage and gave a little speech thanking everyone for their participation. She said that together we had raised thirty-two thousand dollars for breast-cancer research. Everyone clapped and cheered. I felt it should have been so much more — at least a million dollars or so.

The brim of a large straw sun hat hit me on the arm as someone squeezed in and sat down next to me. Elsa lowered her sunglasses and winked at me. She adjusted her beautiful sun hat and put her matching straw bag on the grass between us.

"What are you doing here?" I whispered.

"I never miss a fundraiser," she whispered back, looking around. "Where's the guy with the champagne and the little sandwiches?"

"It's not that kind of fundraiser," I said.

Elsa looked around. "What kind of fundraiser is this? Everyone's sweaty and dressed … the same." She looked bewildered.

"Shhh," I whispered.

On stage, the woman was introducing a breast-cancer survivor named Nina who wanted to share her story with the audience. She was a beautiful, tall woman with long brown hair and small round glasses. She spoke with a soothing voice about the importance of positive thinking and how it helped her so much in her fight against cancer. She said that meditation and yoga were two of the things that kept her strong and focused on healing. She was very graceful and she never stopped smiling.

Elsa nudged me. "I think she's beautiful, don't you?"

I nodded, watching the way the woman looked at the crowd so warmly. She was saying that now that she's well, she teaches yoga to patients and survivors of breast cancer.

Elsa nudged me again. "I think you should go to track-and-field camp this summer," she whispered.

"You came all the way here to tell me that?" I said.

"Do you have a better plan?" she asked.

"Why are you suddenly acting like my running coach?" I whispered.

"Because your running coach is acting like your aunt's boyfriend."

I started to reply, but Elsa put a finger to her lips and pointed to the woman on stage, who was now thanking her daughter Allison for her support. She told her daughter to stand up. A girl in the front stood up and looked shyly around. The women clapped and smiled at her. At first I couldn't tell for sure, but then I knew it. It was the girl from the lingerie department! The one with the brown ponytail; the one who had won my race! I looked over at Elsa to tell her, but she was gone. A dried pink flower from her sun hat was on the grass where she'd been sitting. I put it in the pocket of my shorts.

After the speeches, I looked everywhere for the girl, but all the women were standing now and she'd disappeared into the crowd. I had no idea what I would say to her if I found her, but there was something about her that drew me. Maybe it was some sort of sign, the fact that she kept turning up in my life. On the way home in the car, my mom laughed and talked about how much fun the run was. She'd already made a date with her new ex-lawyer friend to meet for coffee. I was happy that she'd finally found someone from her own species to bond with. I agreed with my mom — the race had been fun — but all I could think about was that mysterious girl named Allison.

Chapter 19

The morning Paul left, the sky was grey and dark clouds were hanging so low they seemed to be touching the tops of the trees. I rode my bike over to his house, and by the time I got to his driveway, it was starting to drizzle. I had to put his gift under my jacket to keep it from getting wet. I tucked it into the top of my jeans so I wouldn't have to hang onto it.

Paul's bags were sitting on the pavement next to the car, getting wet. His mom came out of the house carrying a floral cosmetic case. She was wearing jeans and an oversized purple batik T-shirt. Her makeup was smeared and she looked like she'd had a long day even though it was early morning.

"Hello, Clare," she said, looking up at the sky. I heard her cursing under her breath at the weather as she threw her case in the back of the car. Out loud she said, "Wouldn't ya know it, lousy weather."

I started to tell her that it was more pleasant to drive under cloudy skies, something my mom told me once, but she'd already gone back in the house, the screen door slamming behind her. I stood there feeling like a smarty-pants kid.

Paul opened the screen door. He was struggling with a large green duffel bag. He looked so unhappy that I suddenly forgot how annoyed I'd been with him and I wanted to tell him to stay.

"Oh. Hello, Clare," he said.

"Hi," I said. "Here, let me help you with that." I put my bike down and picked up the other end of the duffel. We dragged it to the car.

"Geez, this is heavy. What do you have in here — a body?"

"Sort of," he said. "It's my microscope and all my specimens."

"You're taking a pickled baboon brain to your grandmother's house?"

"Uh-huh," he said, and sighed.

The rain started to come down harder, and for the first time since I'd met him, Paul seemed oblivious to it. We hoisted the duffel into the trunk. Paul added the rest of his wet bags and slammed the lid of the trunk. "I guess that's everything," he said.

I just stood there feeling awkward. Paul's glasses were dotted with rain, but he made no attempt to wipe them. His short-sleeved plaid shirt was getting wet, too.

Paul's mother came out again, carrying a large coffee thermos under her arm. She locked up the house and stood looking up at the windows for a moment. Maybe she was trying to remember if she'd turned off all the lights and appliances or maybe she was just saying good-bye. She was wearing big, dark sunglasses, which looked odd in the rain.

"Okay, Paul," she said. "Let's get going." She opened the car door and got in.

"Well," said Paul. "I guess I'll see you … whenever."

It was true. Neither of us really knew when we would see each other again. There was no point in pretending and making things up like adults do when they say good-bye. Things like: we'll call, we'll write, maybe we could meet somewhere, we'll be back before you know it.

"This is for you," I said, pulling the package out from under my coat. "It's that *Ultimate Spider-Man* you've been looking for. The one featuring Spider-Man as a teenager in the twenty-first century."

He took the package and turned it around in his hands a couple of times. "Where'd you find it?"

"I can't reveal my sources. I'd have to kill you."

Paul smiled. "Wow. Thanks."

"Sure," I said. I was suddenly glad I'd put some thought into his gift.

"I'm sorry I'm not going to be here for your birthday," he said, digging into his jacket pocket. "Here's a gift. It's really nothing, but promise me you won't open it till your birthday, okay?" He handed me a small square package wrapped in tissue paper with a pale pink ribbon on it. I tried to imagine Paul carefully tying the ribbon into a bow.

Paul's mother tooted the horn. She leaned over to the passenger side and rolled down the window. "Come on, Paul!" she said. "I'd like to beat the worst of this." She gestured at the sky as though there was a tornado approaching or something.

"I'm coming," said Paul. "Well, Clare, have a great summer, okay?"

"You, too," I said, trying to smile. I really wanted to say so much more. I wanted to apologize for not appreciating his friendship and for treating him like a consolation prize just because there was no one better around. I knew now that Paul was being the best friend that someone like Paul can be.

Paul got in the car and his mother slowly backed out of the driveway, straining in her dark glasses to see out the rain-covered windows. She narrowly missed the neighbour's metal garbage cans lining the curb. Paul waved self-consciously as the car started up the street. I waved back and watched the car disappear around the corner.

I stood in the empty driveway holding the little rain-spattered package in my hands. I slowly untied the ribbon and pulled off the tissue paper. I hadn't really promised I wouldn't open it till my birthday, and besides, Paul would never know.

It was a small wooden picture frame. Inside the frame was a picture of Paul and me. We'd taken it in a photo booth at the miniature golf course on the first day of summer vacation. We were both making hideous faces. I stood there looking at it. Suddenly the sky opened up and it started to pour so it didn't matter if I was crying or not.

Chapter 20

Dear Elsa,

Paul is gone. I thought it would be hard to miss him, but it turned out to be easy. Maybe I'm just feeling sorry for myself because now I'm completely alone for the rest of the summer. Track-and-field camp seemed like a really crummy idea when I woke up this morning, so I called the number on the brochure again to try and get out of it. I got the same woman as before. I told her there had been a change in my plans and I asked her if I could get a refund. She said there were absolutely no refunds issued at this late date. I said, "What if someone died?" She said that was a different story and she asked me who died. I said, "No one, I was just checking." I guess I'm going. It starts tomorrow. I suppose you already knew that, since you were the one who was so keen on me going. I swear, Elsa, you really are turning into Mr. Bianchini (except you're not dating my aunt and you didn't tear my heart out). Well, at least Ginny Germain won't be there. She went to some la-di-da summer resort with her family. I might be the fastest runner there, but who'll be watching?

I have to go lie down now. I'm very tired.

Who cares?

Clare

P.S. It's been raining non-stop for two days. The backyard is a swimming hole.

I put the letter down and stared at my bedroom ceiling for a while. My dad was at work and my mom was out with that ex-lawyer woman she met at the breast-cancer run. Even my mom is better than me at making friends now.

I sat up on my elbows and looked around my room. It was shocking, really. There were piles of junk everywhere. Clothes, comic books, magazines and toys I hadn't even looked at in months covered every inch of carpet space. I decided to turn my world upside down.

I started with the clothes. I picked everything up off the floor and separated it into dirty, clean and reject. My underwear drawer was stuffed full, which was one of the reasons I'd started using the floor. I pulled the drawer out and turned it upside down. There were panties in there I hadn't worn since I was six; I put them all on the reject pile along with Wednesday and Saturday, the only two days left of my "Days-of-the-Week" underwear collection. They were looking very frayed and sad. I put the "keepers" back in the drawer and slid it into place. I decided to rename it my "lingerie" drawer (note to self: buy some underwear that actually looks like lingerie).

Next, I folded all my T-shirts and sweatshirts and organized them from favourite to least favourite. I moved my black T-shirts to my least favourite section, naturally.

I picked up all my comic books off the floor and sorted them into separate boxes for Japanese manga, superheroes, and assorted alternative. Then I alphabetized them. When I went to put them back in my closet, an avalanche of stuff came piling out onto me, so I decided to clean that up, too.

I gathered up all the toys off the floor of my closet, then I separated them into appropriate shoe boxes: yo-yos and Hacky Sacks and marbles in one box, and Pez dispensers and action figures in another, and so on. Fortunately, my mom's obsession with shoes means I have an unending supply of boxes.

I worked feverishly, labelling all the boxes with my dad's file labels and a magic marker. I found a bunch of old dolls that were gifts from various relatives who obviously don't know me very well. The dolls were wearing ridiculous little party dresses. Elsa had loved them. One of them had a tan and she was wearing a fluorescent pink bathing suit. I pulled the string on the back of her neck. She said, "Let's go to the beach!" I pulled it again. She said it again. "It's raining, stupid," I said, and I twisted her head off. I pulled the string again. She said it again, but now it was faster, more of a squeak, really. I pulled all the other doll's heads off and put them in a small box that I labelled "Heads," then I put all the bodies in a shoe box that I labelled "Bodies."

Amongst the rubble, I found the china tea set from "Gangster Tea Party" held together with crazy glue. I also found the dress-up clothes and the plastic machine gun. I put them in a larger box that I labelled "Saturdays with Elsa." Then I reconsidered and crossed out the "with Elsa" part.

Things were really starting to come together. You could actually see the carpet, and my closet was completely organized. I even hauled out the vacuum cleaner and vacuumed. I found enough change to buy a new comic book. I put it in a large porcelain piggy bank shaped like Bugs Bunny I'd found in my closet.

When I was finally finished, I sat down on my bed and admired my work. My bedroom was totally unrecognizable. I took one last look and went downstairs.

I was lying on the big green overstuffed sofa, face down, contemplating the big journey into the kitchen to search for some well-deserved ice cream, when the phone rang. It was right next to me on the coffee table, so I felt around for it and picked it up.

"Hello?" I said. My words came out muffled because I still had my face in the sofa cushion.

"Clare?" It was Aunt Rusty. "Why do you sound so funny?"

"Clare isn't in at the moment," I said. "May I take a message?"

"Knock it off. I know it's you."

"All right, it's me, so what?" I rolled over onto my back.

"What are you doing?" she asked.

"Nothing," I said.

"Nothing at all?"

"Well, let's see," I said. "I've decapitated all my old dolls and it isn't even noon yet."

"Well, that's something," she said.

"Is Mr. Bianchini there?" I asked.

"No."

"Did you break up?" I asked hopefully, already planning ways to console poor, heartbroken Mr. Bianchini.

"No. He's just not here all the time."

What my Aunt Rusty fails to understand is that the very idea that Mr. Bianchini comes over there at all is enough to send me over the edge.

"Oh, well in that case, I think there's something you should know. I've been meaning to tell you, but I had to get you alone."

"That's a bit dramatic isn't it, Clare? Just tell me."

"You can't tell anyone. You have to promise me."

"Yeah sure, I promise," Aunt Rusty said, impatiently. "Now tell me."

"Are you sitting down?" I asked.

"Yes!"

"Well, hardly anyone knows this, but Mr. Bianchini used to be married to a beautiful Danish woman named, um, Gretta."

"Gretta?" she said doubtfully. "He never mentioned a Gretta."

"Yes, Gretta. Now listen carefully. One day Gretta mysteriously disappeared and no one saw her for weeks. The neighbours started asking questions, because not only had Gretta vanished, but Mr. Bianchini was acting really strange. He'd be up all night burying things in the backyard and stuff like that."

"Clare …"

"Wait. So one day the woman who lives next door calls her dog in from the backyard. The dog walks in and his paws are all muddy like he's been digging in the dirt and he's got something in his mouth. She walks over to the dog to get a better look and suddenly she starts screaming." I paused for effect. "It was a hand with Gretta's wedding ring on the middle finger."

I waited for a reaction. Nothing. "Aunt Rusty? Are you still there?" I asked.

"And then what?" she said.

"Whaddya mean?" I said.

"Well, what happened after that?"

"Nothing. No one could prove anything. He must have got scared and moved the body."

"I have to talk to Len about this," she said.

"You promised me you wouldn't tell anyone!"

"Did I?" she asked.

"I think you should break up with him right away. If he finds out that you know the truth about him, he might kill you to shut you up."

"Um, Clare?" she said.

"Yeah?"

"You're a lunatic. Are you ever going to forgive me for dating Len?"

"Would you mind calling him Mr. Bianchini? And no, I'm not."

"Don't forget, if you forgive me before your birthday, you get a gift."

"That's bribery and I don't accept bribes, but just for the record, what would the gift be?" I asked.

"What do you want?"

"Same thing I always want. A dog," I said.

"A big one or a small one?"

I thought for a second. "A puppy, but one that gets big."

"Okay," she said. "See you at the party. Bye."

She hung up before I could ask, "What party?"

Chapter 21

The rain stopped just in time for the first day of track-and-field camp. I rode my bike to school, swerving around the puddles and making a game of it as I tried to muster up some enthusiasm. Even though I was furious with Mr. Bianchini, I guess I wasn't quite prepared for someone besides him to be holding the stopwatch.

I left my bike in the racks, which were almost empty. I automatically went for the same spot I use when school is in. I didn't bother locking the bike. It's definitely seen better days. No one would bother stealing a bike in this condition, and if they did, they needed it more than I did.

I walked toward the group of kids gathering near the sports field. They were all boys except for a girl from my grade named Tammy Doherty, who was sitting on the grass alone, wearing a yellow polka-dot ensemble. I was surprised to see her there; I'd never realized she had any interest in track and field. I remember her running into a tree during P.E. in sixth grade and knocking out a tooth. Elsa always called her "Pebbles" (you know, from *The Flintstones*) because she wears her hair in a little ribbon on top of her head. I'd have thought she'd be happier at Barbie camp or Smurf camp. Maybe she didn't have anything else to do with her summer. I could relate to that. She waved at me and I said hello, and then I followed some other newcomers to sign in.

Some more girls trickled in while I was signing in. They were eighth graders, and they looked like serious runners, something I was grateful for. I didn't want to spend the next two weeks playing patty-cake with Tammy.

The instructors were talking amongst themselves. The only one I recognized was Mr. Duffy, the other P.E. teacher at our school. He wasn't even in the same ballpark as Mr. Bianchini looks-wise. He blew his whistle sharply to get everyone's attention. I remembered that he likes to use his whistle a lot; in fact, he rarely takes it out of his mouth. He's always a little red in the face. I guess it's from all that blowing.

Mr. Duffy blew his whistle again. "Hello, I'm Mr. Duffy. I'm one of the instructors for this camp. Let's all sit down and get acquainted."

I found a place in the back. The grass was still damp from the rain, so I took off my jacket and sat on it. Mr. Duffy was introducing the other two instructors. He started with Ms. Steele, who got enthusiastic applause. I guess she was pretty popular at the school where she taught. She was very tall and skinny and a bit scary. Mr. Duffy also introduced Mr. Kelly, who only got polite clapping. He looked like a nice man to me. Maybe none of his students had come to the camp. Maybe they had lives.

Mr. Duffy continued, "We'd like to welcome you and tell you a bit about this camp. First of all, it's going to be a lot of fun."

Wheeeee! I thought. *I'm having fun already!*

I'm very skeptical of people who have to tell you that something's going to be fun instead of just letting it be fun. They're the same people who always say, "That's funny" instead of just laughing.

"We'll start each day with a good stretch and then everyone will run a warm-up mile, not just the runners." Everyone groaned. "I know, I know," he said, "but the good news is that every day we'll play a new game for prizes." Everyone cheered and Tammy put her hand up.

"Yes?" said Mr. Duffy.

"Um, are the prizes going to be food? Because, if they are, I have a list of my food allergies."

"Okay, you can see me later about that."

"Oh, okay, 'cause I can swell up like a balloon and one time my throat closed. I almost died."

"Okay, let's move on then," said Mr. Duffy.

He went on for some time about good sportsmanship and rules and stuff like that. I gazed off into the distance and watched an old blue Volkswagen van pull up in front of the school. A girl got out the passenger side and looked anxiously toward us. She said something to the driver and slammed the van door. The van pulled away from the curb and drove off. I recognized the girl's gait as she sprinted toward our group. I'd know that long brown ponytail anywhere. It was the girl I'd been thinking about. It was Allison.

She was wearing a white T-shirt with Elvis Costello on the front and carrying a bottle of water and an army surplus canvas bag. She dropped her things on the grass right next to my hand and mumbled, "Sorry" to Mr. Duffy, who had stopped speaking while she got settled. She sat down next to me and Mr. Duffy continued.

"Did I miss anything?" she whispered to me. I turned to face her and she recognized me.

"Hey, I know you!" she said, loudly enough to turn everyone's head in our direction.

"Yeah, I know you, too," I said, suddenly shy.

"I'm Allison," she said, remembering to whisper.

"Clare," I said.

"Clare. That's a cool name."

"Ugh, but thanks. I like yours, too."

"I changed it. It used to be Serenity." She rolled her eyes. "My parents were hippies."

"You can change your name?" I asked. "I didn't know that."

Mr. Duffy blew his whistle, startling us. "Girls, is there anything you'd like to share with the group?"

Everyone turned around to stare at us.

"Sorry," we both said.

"Okay," said Mr. Duffy, "please pay attention."

We grinned at each other.

When Mr. Duffy finally wrapped it up, the instructors divided us into groups according to the events we were best at. Allison and I were in the same group. I was delighted. Ms. Steele was our coach. She led our group of about fifteen through a series of stretches. She had a sing-songy way of talking that reminded me of a nursery school teacher who had terrified me. Allison and I looked like a couple of flamingos with our right legs pulled up behind us in a quadricep stretch.

"So, do you have a boyfriend?" asked Allison.

"No," I answered. "Do you?" We changed from our right legs to our left.

"No. Boys don't like me," she said matter-of-factly. "I'm not worried about it, though. I'm not ready for a commitment. Besides, I'm hoping to date older men when the time comes."

"Like who?" I asked.

Allison blew a wisp of hair out of her face. "I dunno, no one I've met yet. Maybe an artist or a poet or something."

"Ugh, artists. My aunt's an artist."

"Don't you like her?"

"Well, I did, but it's a long story."

"Oh," Allison shrugged. "Okay."

We got down on the ground to do a hurdler's stretch and I changed the subject. "Do you have any brothers or sisters?" I asked.

"I have an older brother, but he doesn't live at home. He's in college. I can't stand him; he's a moron. How about you?"

"No, there's just me."

"You're lucky. I tell most people I'm an only child."

Ms. Steele instructed us to lay on our backs and sang out orders as we stretched out our backs. Allison and I lay side by side, looking up at the retreating clouds in the sky.

"Is your family dysfunctional?" asked Allison.

I laughed. "Yes. Is yours?"

"Completely. But they pretend they're not."

After we finished stretching, we ran the mile together. Since we weren't racing, it was easy to talk while we jogged. I asked Allison where she lived.

"At the Holiday Inn," she said.

"What?"

"The Holiday Inn. My parents sold our house and the new one isn't ready yet. My dad's building it himself. He's making it all self-contained and solar-heated like the biosphere, except we get to come out. He's a first-class kook."

"Where's the house going to be?" I asked.

"Right near here, on Pine. I'm going to this school next year."

"Me, too!"

"I know. I saw your T-shirt at the district track meet. I put two and two together." She turned to me and crossed her eyes.

"Why didn't you say something?"

"I don't know. I didn't want you to think I was a geek or something."

"I wouldn't have," I said. "I saw you at that breast-cancer run last weekend and I thought the same thing. I couldn't think of anything clever to say to you."

"Really, you were there? Man, that was embarrassing. You should have come over. What a couple of goofballs we are," she said, wiping her forehead with her hand.

"No kidding," I said.

"Do you have a best friend at this school?" she asked.

"No," I said. "I'm kind of between best friends right now."

"Yeah, me, too," she grinned. "Not that I haven't had friends in the past, I'm not a psychopath or anything. My last best friend's dad was a gangster and now her family's in the witness protection program and I can't even contact her."

"Really?" I asked.

Allison shrugged. "No. I saw that on TV; it's way more exciting than what really happened. Her dad got transferred."

"My best friend moved to Europe," I said.

"Wow, that's pretty far. Is she ever coming back?"

"I'm not sure," I said.

Before we knew it, we'd finished the mile easily. The rest of the day flew by and I was sorry to see it end. Allison walked with me to get my bike at the racks and we wheeled it over to the curb where her mom was supposed to pick her up.

"She'll be late," said Allison. "She's always late."

While we waited, we sucked on the grape Popsicles that Mr. Duffy had given everyone. (Well, everyone but Tammy, who was quick to inform us all that she's allergic to the dye in popsicles … sheesh!) Allison got a pen out of her book bag and wrote the phone number of the Holiday Inn on a scrap of paper. She wrote "Room 320" underneath the number. She gave me another scrap of paper for my number.

Her mom finally drove up in the van. Allison pretended to be hitchhiking. She got in the van and rolled down the window. Her mom smiled at me and Allison introduced us.

"Call me tonight, okay?" she said.

"Sure," I said, "what time?"

"Um, how about around six fifty-nine?"

Allison's mom pulled away from the curb and Allison waved goodbye.

I waved back. I watched the van travel up the street and tried to read all the bumper stickers on the back bumper: THINK GREEN, RECYCLE, SUPPORT ORGANIC FARMING, and THE GRATEFUL DEAD. I smiled and got on my bike.

Chapter 22

When I got home from camp, there was a postcard from Paul waiting for me on the hall table. I went into the kitchen, said hi to my mom and poured myself a glass of lemonade. I sat down at the kitchen table to read the postcard. My mom sat across from me. Her right foot was up on the table and she had stuffed a wad of toilet paper between each toe. She was painting her toenails while she watched the Naked Chef make a lemon *soufflé*. I happen to know my mom is afraid of *soufflés*. The fact that they could fall is way too much of a risk factor for her.

The front of the postcard was a faded picture of a Hawaiian girl in a grass skirt doing the hula. The edges were torn and yellowing. Across the top it said "Aloha from Hawaii" in red writing. I turned the postcard over. The writing was so tiny that I had to hold it right up to my face to read it.

Dear Clare,

I'm not in Hawaii. Not even close. I found this postcard in my grandmother's "card file," where she keeps greeting cards, circa 1948, for all occasions. It explains the weird birthday cards I've received over the years. My grandmother's motto is "Always Be Prepared." Speaking of being prepared, I also found a large cardboard box filled with twenty-dollar bills in the closet underneath a lifetime supply of toilet paper. It's possible that neither of my grandparents remember it's there. I'm guessing they don't, because every year I get a crisp five-dollar bill inside my vintage birthday card. My grandparents stockpile groceries from a place called "Liquidation World" and they haven't been to a real supermarket in this century, so they're probably unaware of the sharply rising cost of living. Their idea of splurging is buying hot chocolate mix with marshmallows.

My grandparents live in a minimum-security prison compound for old people. The security guards are all eighty years old and drive riding lawn mowers. You can only get into this place if you can prove you've lost your marbles (they both passed with flying colours). You can only get out if you die. They haven't had a conversation with each other since 1972 and they'll tell anyone who'll listen that they can't stand each other. My grandmother will only cook food that comes in a can because she thinks fresh food is "unsanitary." Most of the cans are dented because they come from "Liquidation World." Are you getting the picture?

I met a guy named Klaus (I'm not kidding), who lives across the street from "The Compound." It turns out we share a lot of interests: chemistry, biology, genetics, forensics. He accelerated in school, so he's fourteen and starting tenth grade in September. He actually has his own laboratory in his basement with test mice and everything. We're conducting a little DNA experiment, but I'll tell you more about that later. You never know who reads these postcards.

Another perk is that his mom cooks real food, so I try to hang around at dinnertime. Things aren't quite as dismal as I thought they would be . . . yet. I even found a comic book store and I just picked up New X-Men. I hope you're having an excellent summer. Happy birthday. Write when you can.

Paul

There was no return address.

"How's Paul?" asked my mom as I set the postcard down on the table.

"Great," I said. "He made a friend."

My mom's eyebrows arched. "A girl?"

"No. A boy. His name is Klaus. He sounds like another genius. Imagine Paul meeting someone who's as strange as he is; what are the chances of that?"

"You'd think zero." My mom changed feet and rolled up toilet paper to stuff between the toes on her left foot. "Tell me about camp," she said.

I spoke nonchalantly. "It was great, actually. Speaking of friends, remember the girl who beat me in the district finals?"

"Sure, the girl with the long brown ponytail?"

"Right. Well, she's in my camp and she's going to my school next year."

"Clare, that's wonderful!"

I knew she'd be pleased. She likes to hang on to any shred of evidence that I might actually be normal and capable of making a friend. I went to the fridge for more lemonade. I almost tripped over a box and three large wardrobe bags sitting by the back kitchen door.

"What are these?" I asked my mom.

"Suits, career clothes, stuff I don't need anymore. I'm giving them to a women's shelter."

"You're giving that stuff away? Does that mean you're never going back to work?"

"Well, no. Let's just say that I'm never going back to the kind of work where you have to wear a suit and panty-hose." She looked up from her toes and smiled at me.

"You didn't put your old pantyhose in those bags, did you?"

"No, honey, those I'm saving for you."

"Gee, thanks. They'll come in handy for my next bank heist." I opened the fridge and got out the lemonade pitcher.

"Clare," said my mom, "why don't you invite your new friend to your birthday pa ..." She trailed off.

I spun around. "A party? You promised me — no parties!"

"It's not a party; it's just us."

"Us who?" I asked suspiciously.

"Just us and Aunt Rusty," she said.

"And Mr. Bianchini?"

"I don't know, maybe." She looked sheepish.

"Well, he can't come. It's MY birthday."

"Clare, I doubt he'll come anyway, but we can't be rude."

"Yes, we can. People are rude all the time, you even said so."

"Okay," she sighed, "but if you don't want him here, you can call your aunt yourself and tell her."

"Okay, I will," I said, knowing I probably wouldn't. I didn't want my mom to feel bad about any of this. It wasn't her fault that Aunt Rusty had decided to ruin everything. Meeting Allison was changing my perspective, too. I had a feeling that Allison might agree with me if I told her the whole story, even though we barely knew each other. I felt strangely connected to her, as though I'd known her in another life and some outside force was pushing us together in this one. Of course, I would never tell her that; it's way too "New-Age Sensitive" and not something you tell the love child of two hippies.

After dinner, I took the phone up to my room and shut the door. It was five minutes to seven. I took the slip of paper with Allison's number on it out of my pocket and looked at it. Her writing was really messy; the numbers looked as though a six-year-old had written them. I waited until five minutes past seven before I dialed the number. I was trying not to look too desperate.

The hotel operator answered, "Good evening. Holiday Inn."

"Hello," I said, "room three-twenty please." The operator connected me and the phone rang a couple of times.

"Hello?" It was Allison's mom.

"Hello," I said. "Is Allison there?"

"May I ask who's calling?" she asked.

"It's Clare," I said. "From camp."

"Oh, hi, Clare. Allison told me you'd be calling. She's in the pool and she said she'll call you the second she gets out, okay?"

"Sure, thank you." I hung up. I took it as a good sign that she was expecting my call, maybe even looking forward to it. I sat there staring at the phone. When it rang I jumped four feet. I picked it up on the second ring.

"Hello?" I said.

"Clare?"

"Yes?"

"It's Allison."

"Oh, hi." I tried to sound casual. "How was your swim?" I heard a dog barking in the background.

"Hang on a sec. Shut up, Elvis!" she yelled. "Sorry about that."

"You have a dog?" I asked.

"Yeah, Elvis."

"Like the King?"

"No, the other Elvis. Elvis Costello. I'm a big fan."

"I love dogs," I said. I immediately felt stupid. I would

rather have said something smart about Elvis Costello, but I didn't know anything about him.

"Really?" she said. "How about turtles, rats and rabbits?"

"Sure, I love all animals, why?"

"'Cause I've got those, too. I keep the turtle in the bath- tub and the rat and the rabbits out on the balcony. Hotel housekeeping is counting the minutes until I'm gone. Oh, and guess what? I have great news."

"What?"

"We're moving into the new house on Friday. I can finally say good riddance to hotel hell."

"That's great. Is it finished?"

"Not really, but my dad can do the rest while we're in there. He'll probably be building it for the rest of his life, anyway."

"I can help if you like," I said.

"Build the house?"

"No, I meant I could help you move. I'm really good with boxes."

"Hey, that would be great! I can't wait. I'm so sick of living out of a suitcase and Mrs. Spinelli, I call her Mrs. Smelly, she is so sick of me and my pets. Last week one of the rats got out."

"Did you find it?" I asked.

"Eventually. He was in the room next door. He scared the pants off the guy staying there, naughty rat. I'm just happy the poor little guy didn't fall off the balcony.

Mrs. Smelly went ballistic. I told her she should take down the 'Pets Welcome' sign, or at least specify which pets are welcome."

I started to laugh at the image of a rat running around between some guy's feet. Allison started to laugh, too.

"Yeah, I guess it is pretty funny when you think about it," she said.

Our conversation was going pretty well. I decided it was time for a bold move. "What are you doing this weekend?" I asked.

"Hmm, let's see, moving, moving and did I mention, we're moving?"

"Well, it's my birthday on Saturday and my mom's having a little get-together. It's no big deal, just the family, but if you're not doing anything ..."

"Will there be party favours?" she asked.

"Of course, and ice cream and cake and pin the tail on the donkey."

"Are dogs allowed?"

"Absolutely, and you have to wear a party dress," I said.

"Shoot, all my party dresses are still packed," Allison said, suddenly adopting a southern accent. "Nevah mind, I'll sew me a new one! I've got yawds and yawds of peach chiffon."

I started laughing again. No one but Elsa could ever make me laugh like this before.

"Clare, there's something else you should know about me."

"What?" I said anxiously.

"Relax, I haven't been to prison or anything, it's just that I'm a, a … oh, this is so hard." She paused, keeping me in suspense.

"A kleptomaniac?" I said.

"No."

"Pyromaniac?"

"No."

"Serial killer?"

"No, it's much worse," she said dramatically. "I'm a vegetarian."

"Oh, darn," I said, mimicking the drama. "How will it ever work? I'm a cannibal."

"Well, it was nice knowin' ya."

I laughed. "Don't worry about it. My mom will be thrilled. She loves pulverizing vegetables in her new food processor."

"Great. Pulverized vegetables happen to be my favourite food."

For the next hour, I lay on my stomach on my bed, tracing designs with my finger on the carpet below, talking to Allison about absolutely everything (except Elsa, of course). She told me what it was like when her mom had cancer and I told her what it was like to be an only child with two lawyers for parents. It was getting dark outside when my mom came into my room and gave me a get-off-the-phone look. I told Allison I had to hang up and we arranged to meet at the bike racks the next morning. After I hung up the phone, I suddenly realized who Allison reminded me of. It was Elsa.

Chapter 23

I kicked off my birthday with some serious mirror time. I got out of bed and went directly into the bathroom, locking the door behind me. I stared at my face in the mirror, feature by feature, looking for any sign of a change. Then I went back into my room and dug out my sixth-grade school photo. I brought that into the bathroom and held it next to my face in the mirror. The changes weren't drastic, but my face as a whole had changed a lot since sixth grade. For one thing, all the baby fat was gone. My face wasn't round anymore. It was longer and narrower and I looked more mature, somehow. I pulled off my bathrobe and dropped it on the floor. I stood in front of the mirror in my nightshirt. My body looked longer almost everywhere: legs, arms, waist, feet. If I didn't know better, I'd say I was turning into a chimp. Even my hair was longer. It seemed to grow daily. I'd actually purchased my first ponytail holders. My ponytail was long enough that I could sometimes feel it touch the back of my neck when I moved my head. I purposely moved my head more because I liked the way it felt.

Maybe it was a good thing my body was changing so slowly. It was giving me a chance to get used to it. Aunt Rusty was right, I guess, when she told me I shouldn't be in such a rush to grow up. What's the big deal about it, anyway?

I put my bathrobe on and went back into my room to get dressed. My bedroom smelled of French perfume and my bed, which had been unmade when I left the room, was now made. It was also covered in pink rose petals that spelled "Happy Birthday." In the middle of the bed was a tiny box from a parfumerie called "Lavande" on the *Rue du Faubourg St. Honoré* in Paris. I opened it up. Inside was a tiny glass vial of perfume called "*Violette*." I pulled out the stopper and dabbed my wrists; the perfume smelled like sweet violets. It was the scent I had noticed on Elsa. Had I really thought she would miss my birthday? I tucked the perfume into my new lingerie drawer.

I went downstairs to find an empty kitchen. The counters were full of half-prepared dishes and open cookbooks. I was a little annoyed. I had expected more fanfare than this. It was my birthday, after all. Then I noticed the note on the fridge. It said "Happy Birthday, Clare! We'll be right back." There was a stack of birthday cards on the counter from my Aunt Beth, my Uncle Tom and my grandparents on both sides, who live in retirement communities on opposite sides of the country. I tore the cards open and lined them up on the counter. My Grandma Barbara, who smells like oatmeal, sent me fifty dollars, and my Grandma Susan, who smells like roses, sent me a hundred dollars. I stacked it up like Monopoly money and fantasized about packing up my things and heading out on the open highway, but I knew my mom would make me put the money in the bank for college and I don't know how to drive anyway.

I poured myself a bowl of cereal, drowned it in milk, and sat down at the kitchen table to eat. I thought about the last few days. I'd spent almost every waking moment with Allison. My mom even let me take the day off camp to help Allison move into her new house. It's the coolest house I've ever seen. The walls are filled with straw bales and everything is made out of something recycled. Allison's family has all kinds of energy-saving gadgets, even a solar-powered oven! The rooms are airy and cool and uncluttered. It felt peaceful, even though Elvis was running from room to room, checking the place out.

Allison loved my house. She thought all the creaks and squeaks were charming and she loved the idea that someone may have died in it. Her favourite part was the roof. We climbed out there just as a storm was approaching one night to watch the lightning zigzag across the sky. We counted one one-thousand, two one-thousand, three one-thousand before the thunder clapped. We couldn't tell anyone we were out there because my dad is certain that lightning is going to strike the tree next to the house, splitting it in half, and then the tree is going to crash onto the roof, squashing me like a bug. What he doesn't know won't hurt him. We sat out there until the rain came pouring down on us. I'd never sat on the roof with anyone but Elsa before.

I met Allison's dad and I liked him right away. He's sort of weird, but in a good way. He's tall with friendly blue eyes and he calls Allison "Al." He's an environmental engineer and Allison's mom is a social worker. Allison looks a lot like her mom. She has the kind of face that becomes prettier as you know her better. Most people would call it "interesting," but I hate that because I think it means that you don't look like what most people call "pretty."

I decided to invite Allison's parents to my party because I thought they would be a good influence on my parents. I thought maybe they could teach my parents how to compost or something. My mom was in favour of having them to dinner, but it sent her into a flurry of preparations, especially when she found out they were vegetarians. You'd have thought I'd said they were Klingons. She was even more confused when I told her that Allison's parents weren't married. Apparently they don't believe in it so they simply made a promise to each other on a beach somewhere in Mexico. I'm sure one of the many thoughts flying through my mother's head was that if we all behaved this way, there would be no work for the divorce lawyers.

My mom's vast and ever-growing collection of kitchen equipment now rivalled Martha Stewart's. Her food library had grown so much that she had to put the overflow in the dining room (she happily banished my entire collection of encyclopedias to the basement in boxes). The kitchen cupboards were bulging with ingredients. I had to dig through jars of pickled peppercorns, anchovies, capers and things I'd never heard of to get to my peanut butter. She even tried to make peanut butter herself with her food processor. It tasted like dirt. I had to put my foot down. The stuff from the supermarket with the squirrels on the front is good enough for me.

I had to admit that I was sort of getting used to having my mom around and it was kind of nice to see her fussing over my birthday like this. It sure beat eating a fast dinner in a restaurant and then blushing as the waiter slapped down a stale piece of cake with a lit candle in front of me and he and the busboys sang "Happy Birthday, Dear Customer."

As I rescued the last few bits of cereal floating in the milk like tiny life preservers, it occurred to me that camp would be over in a week and I still hadn't managed to beat Allison in even one race. It was always so close and I knew that I should be happy just to keep up with her. My times were great but I just wanted to beat her once. Allison had absolutely no ego about being such a good runner. It didn't even seem to mean that much to her. I really didn't think it would bother her if I won. I had one more week and I was determined to do it.

I heard the car in the driveway and my mom came in a few minutes later yelling, "Happy Birthday!" and trying to hide a large pink cake box as though I would have absolutely no idea what was inside it. My dad was mysteriously absent.

"Thanks," I said. "Where's Dad?"

"Oh, he'll be right in. He's checking on something in the garage."

Clearly this was where my gift was. My dad never went in the garage.

"He's hiding my gift, isn't he?" I asked.

"No," she lied.

"Should I bring out a bowl of water in case my gift gets thirsty?"

"No. It's not a dog. It's better."

"A pony?"

"Clare." She shot me a look.

"Sorry," I said.

My mom got to work cleaning enough vegetables for fifty people. She washed and dried some eggplants. Then she sliced them up and put them in a strainer in the sink. She went to the fridge and pulled out some more exotic vegetables and started washing them. I sat on a stool at the counter and watched. She looked at me and smiled.

Chapter 24

Allison and her parents arrived at my birthday party fifteen fashionable minutes late, at 2:45 p.m. My dad and I were on the back deck. I was showing him how to light the barbecue. Elvis beat everyone into the back-yard, so he was the first to wish me a happy birthday. He licked my face with his big wet tongue and ran off to explore the yard. My dad looked on disapprovingly until I assured him that Elvis was very well-trained. Allison came around the corner next, followed by her parents. She was carrying a round glass fishbowl with turquoise gravel on the bottom and a little goldfish swimming around in it. She handed it to me.

"Happy Birthday," she said. "Her name is Maude. Don't feed her too much; I've heard they can become enormous."

I took the bowl and peered in at the little fish. "Thanks," I said. "She's beautiful."

"Welcome to the world of pets. I remember my first goldfish."

"Hi, Maude," I said to the fish. "I'm Clare." I held the bowl toward my dad. "Look, Dad, the perfect pet — she can't get out." My dad didn't look convinced.

"Oh, and here." Allison dug a CD out of her canvas bag and put it in my free hand. "This is an introduction to Elvis Costello."

My mom came out and everyone introduced themselves. Allison's parents were really friendly and it wasn't even a little bit awkward. My mom had tied helium balloons to the railing of the deck and taped one of those cheesy plastic HAPPY BIRTHDAY banners to the side of the garage. She brought out a giant tray of veggies and dip. Allison told her parents to behave themselves and we went up to my room so I could show her some of my new comic books.

I yanked the tidy boxes out of my closet and set them on the floor next to the bed. We kicked off our sandals and sat on the bed digging through them. Allison was already hooked, even though she'd just started collecting. I showed her some of my old stuff that was out of print, the stuff Paul made me buy. Allison relaxed with my Spider-Man pillow behind her head and a stack of comic books next to her. She was the first girl I'd ever met who actually got as excited as I did about comic books. She seemed to like the alternative stuff the best, but she also liked the classics, especially Catwoman and Batgirl. She already knew all of the superheroes by heart. Paul would have loved her.

I recognized the noisy rumble of Aunt Rusty's convertible approaching. I jumped off the bed and ran to the window. Aunt Rusty was pulling up to the curb in front of the house. There was someone in the seat next to her. My heart sank. Allison joined me at the window.

"Who is it?" she asked.

"It's my Aunt Rusty, and she brought Mr. Bianchini. I'll kill her!" I threw myself on my bed, scattering comic books. "I can't go down there. I can't face him. Go tell them that I have food poisoning or I jumped out the window or something."

Allison looked out the window again. "Wow," she said, "Mr. Bianchini's pretty short."

I lifted my head. "Huh? He's not short."

"Is he blond?" she asked.

"No. Mr. Bianchini has black hair."

"Does he have four legs?"

I jumped off the bed. "Let me see." I looked down at the car. Aunt Rusty was standing on the passenger side of her car, trying to gather up a very happy golden Labrador puppy. He had a blue ribbon around his neck. She finally managed to wrestle him into her arms. She kicked the car door shut with her foot and started for the backyard. Allison and I looked at each other and charged down the stairs.

We hit the back deck just as Aunt Rusty was rounding the corner with the big puppy trying to scramble out of her arms.

"Happy Birthday," she said, and plopped the puppy into my arms. He licked my face and I sat down on the deck and let him jump all over me. Elvis came over to sniff him and the puppy touched noses with him. My parents looked on in disbelief.

Allison looked around and whispered, "Uh-oh."

"Angela, can I talk to you a second in the kitchen?" said my mom, leading Aunt Rusty roughly by the elbow through the open glass door and sliding it closed behind them. Unfortunately, she forgot to close the window over the sink, so we could hear everything they said.

"What were you thinking?" said my mom. "How could you do something like that without asking us first? You know what your problem is? You don't have any boundaries."

I cringed.

"And you know what yours is?" asked Aunt Rusty, not waiting for an answer. "You have too many."

From outside on the deck, we could actually feel my mom's anger percolating.

"Look," said Aunt Rusty calmly. "The guy I bought it from said I could bring it back if you didn't want it."

"You can't take it away now that you've given it to her!"

"Okay, I won't," said Aunt Rusty. "She's been asking for a dog ever since she could talk. Are you going to deny her one just because someday you might decide to landscape the yard and the dog might dig up a tulip?"

"That's not the point! You are not her fairy godmother. You can't just show up here in a puff of smoke and give her anything she wants and then disappear."

"That's not fair!" yelled Aunt Rusty. "I've never disappeared! And speaking of disappearing, where were you for the first twelve years of her life?!"

My mom said nothing. I admired my aunt's use of guilt as a debating tool.

Meanwhile, out on the deck, things were getting pretty uncomfortable. We were all trying to pretend we weren't listening. Allison's parents didn't say much, but they seemed to be rooting for the puppy. They did, after all, have a menagerie in their house. I could tell my dad was just itching to get in there and put in his two cents' worth, but he knew things were looking bad enough already. What would Allison's parents think if he left them out here to join the scream-fest in the kitchen? I covered the puppy's ears so he wouldn't be traumatized. Elvis came over and sat beside us as though he were offering his support. The puppy squirmed away from me, trotted over to my dad, and looked up at him with his tail wagging. My dad leaned over and patted his soft head and that was all the puppy needed. He was all over my dad.

The yelling continued from the kitchen.

"Even if I did say it was okay, it would have to be okay with Dan, too," said my mom.

"Well, why don't you ask him?" said Aunt Rusty.

"Okay, but I don't like your chances," said my mom.

My mom and Aunt Rusty came back out on the deck in time to see the puppy in my dad's lap, licking his face while my dad laughed and asked, "Who's a good puppy, huh? Who's a good puppy?"

My mom looked at Aunt Rusty and shrugged. Aunt Rusty winked at me.

"Does that mean I can keep him?" I asked, looking at my dad pleadingly.

"Okay," said my dad, still laughing "but he's your responsibility: walking, feeding, training, cleaning up after him, everything."

"All right!" I shouted. Allison and I threw our arms around each other and Elvis jumped up and ran around us barking. The puppy jumped off my dad's lap and joined in. I gave Aunt Rusty a big hug.

"Thank you! This is unbelievable. I love him!" I said.

"Her," she said. "It's a her."

"Her? She's a girl? That's even better!"

"Okay, so we're square, right? All is forgiven?"

"Sure," I said. "Why not?"

"Good. I didn't want to have to offer cash, too."

"Cash?" I said. "How much cash?"

"Don't push your luck. What'll you name her?"

"Elsa," I said, without even thinking about it.

"Good name," said Aunt Rusty, dipping a carrot stick and putting it in her mouth.

"Elsa," said Allison, cuddling the puppy while Elvis looked on from the ground. "Yes. The perfect name for you. Like the lion in *Born Free*."

"Yeah," I said.

My parents seemed to forgive Aunt Rusty, which was a good idea because being mad at Aunt Rusty is pointless (although I did get a dog out of it).

Allison's parents got along great with Aunt Rusty, and

it turned out that they were in the market for a painting for the new house. I wasn't sure they were ready for Aunt Rusty's style, but who was I to say anything? They might love it.

Elsa played with Elvis in the yard until she wore him out and they fell asleep on the deck next to each other. After dinner, my mom and dad brought a new bike out of the garage for me. It was a bright blue twenty-one-speed mountain bike. I still felt sentimentally attached to my old, pathetic bike for some reason. Everything about this birthday was brand new and a part of me was still clinging to the old Clare, the old bike, the old Elsa.

I took the new bike for a spin around the block. Allison rode next to me on my old one. We raced each other back to the house and I cut her off at the pass, going up on the curb and across my front lawn.

My mom brought out a giant chocolate cake with fourteen candles on it (thirteen and one to grow on). Everyone sang "Happy Birthday" and I blew every candle out.

"Did you make a wish?" asked Allison.

"Sure," I said. "But it already came true."

Chapter 25

The gun went off and everyone charged forward. It was the last race of the summer and my last chance to beat Allison, my new best friend. Obviously, I wasn't allowed to make it seem important to me to win and I was a little ashamed of my competitive attitude. Allison's friendship meant so much to me that I would rather stick hot pokers up my nose than jeopardize it.

As we rounded the first corner of the track, I thought about how much my life had changed in the last month. The future, or at least eighth grade, was looking surprisingly bright. I had a whole bunch of new friends; one of them was a dog and another was my mom and even my dad was starting to show signs of being human.

The pounding of sneakers around me jolted me back into the race. I switched into a higher gear and moved ahead of the group. Allison stayed on my right, like she always does, for most of the race. I became conscious of the steady sound of her breathing and how it matched mine exactly. I lost myself in the familiar rhythm of it as though it were a drumbeat we were moving to.

On the second lap of the race, Allison was still on my right, but neither of us said a word to each other. We usually chatted well into the second lap, but this time we both seemed to be taking the race very seriously. As we rounded the last corner, I saw a girl standing alone off to the side of the track. I could tell by the way she was dressed that she wasn't from the camp. She was wearing a long, filmy, sheer green dress that rippled in the breeze. Her feet were bare and her long blonde hair blew behind her as she watched us.

I felt an unexpected burst of energy from somewhere inside me and I inched ahead of Allison. As I approached the finish, I recognized the girl watching us. It was someone I knew as well as I knew myself. It was Elsa.

Time seemed to stand still. I watched Elsa slowly wave to me. She looked happy and sort of peaceful. She turned and started to walk away. Everyone, including Allison, was slapping me on the back and congratulating me, but it took me a moment to realize that I'd won the race. Ms. Steele checked our times and made it official: I'd topped Allison's personal best. I tried to see past all the people for a sign of Elsa — I looked everywhere, but I knew that she was gone.

After the race, camp was officially over. There was a quick awards ceremony and I got the "Purple Heart" award for a spectacular wipe-out I'd taken the week before that left a big scrape on my right knee. Allison got the "Academy Award" for being the most entertaining camper. Afterwards, Allison wanted to go to the Dairy Delite.

"I'll buy," she said. "To the victor go the spoils."

"I can't," I said. "There's something I have to do. It can't wait."

"Let me get this straight. You're turning down a root-beer float?"

"Yeah."

"It's not like you beat me every day, or you ever will again," she said.

"I know," I said. "I just have to do this one thing." I felt on the verge of tears.

Allison seemed to understand. "Well, later then, okay?"

"Sure," I said.

Allison got on her bike and started pedalling toward her street. She looked over her shoulder and smiled. "Call me!" she said.

"I will," I said. I got on my bike and pedalled home. When I opened the front door, Elsa bounded at me. I knelt down and she jumped on me, licking my face. I ran up the stairs with her at my heels. In my room, Maude swam happily around the Eiffel Tower in a glass bowl that sat on my dresser. I put Elsa on the bed with my newly tattered slipper to chew on while I wrote.

Dear Elsa,

I never dreamed that there would be a day when we would say goodbye for real. But I think you knew all along that this was coming, and I realize now that you were pushing me in that direction. You always did seem to know what was best for me. It's hard to let go of something that means as much to me as you do. You are everything that I am and I am everything that you are. How do you say goodbye to someone who's been your best friend for ten years? I can't begin to try. Thank you. I'll never forget you.

Love,
Clare

I put the pen down and closed my eyes. A single tear slowly rolled down my cheek. Elsa licked it off, and I knew that she would always be there.

**Wait ... there's more Clare?
You bet. Look for**

Not Fair,
Clare

available at a bookstore near you!

When you have a black eye, people are instantly nicer to you. It's important to take advantage of the situation. My mom made me an apple pie for dessert, and my dad actually made it home in time to eat dinner with us, which happens about as often as the vernal equinox. My dad was all over the black eye, threatening lawsuits and police action till my mom gave him a look. Somewhere along the way my mom has figured out that if things are going to work between us, she's going to have to stop making a big deal out of everything (she did make me take off the dark sunglasses at the table, though). My dad hasn't quite caught on to the program yet. He has two gears: high and asleep.

While my mom serves up the pie, my dad asks the usual questions.

"How are things at school?"

"Great."

"How's the running? Are you still making good time?"

"I guess, but I'm sort of interested in acting this year."

"You're giving up the track team?" He looks mildly concerned (he wanted a boy).

"I'm still taking Track and Field as a class, but I just want to focus on Drama right now. I'm auditioning for Lady Macbeth at the end of the week."

"Lady Macbeth? Now there's a motivated woman for you. Too bad she goes nuts in the end. The pressure just gets to be too much, I guess." He sighs and takes a sip of coffee.

My mom jumps in. "At least she doesn't lose her head literally. Nothing much has changed in the world. The women do all the thinking and the men do all the fighting."

My dad grunts, which is his standard reaction to a point when he doesn't want to incite a "discussion."

"Did you know that some people think there's a curse on that play?" asks my mom.

"A curse? What do you mean?" I say.

"I'm a little fuzzy on the details, but a lot of productions of the play have been plagued with catastrophes and, um, people dying and being stabbed and set on fire and stuff like that." Her voice trails off as she catches my dad looking at her in alarm.

"Honey, ignore your mom. She doesn't know what she's talking about. It's all just a bunch of theatre folklore."

"Oh, wait. I just remembered," says my mom. "You can avoid the curse by never saying the name of the play in the theatre it's performed in."

"But I already did!"

"Okay. Never mind then. How's that pie taste?"

"How do you guys know so much about *Macbeth*?" I ask.

"I played one of the witches in my college's production," says my mom. "Your dad must have seen the play seventeen times, didn't you, honey?"

My dad clears his throat. "Uh, that isn't entirely true. Most of the time I stayed for your first scene and then went for a couple of beers and came back for the end."

"I know," says my mom. "I always saw you leave. I was just testing you."

"What do you mean 'testing me'? Why do I need to be tested?"

"You don't. I was just checking to see if you could tell the truth after all these years."

"Of course I can. What difference does it make at this point anyway?"

I put my sunglasses on and sit back in my chair with my arms crossed. My mom notices and snaps out of it. My dad looks ready for round two.

"More pie, Clare?" asks my mom in an artificially sweetened voice.

"No, thanks."

My mom glares at my dad and he tries to get back to his line of questioning.

"What happened to that kid you used to hang out with?"

"Who?" I pretend not to know who he's talking about.

"You know, the smart one."

"Allison," says my mom icily. "Her name is Allison."

"No, that's not it. This was a boy. It was Peter, or something with a 'P.'"

"Paul?" I say. "You're talking about Paul? Dad, Paul's been gone for months. He left in July!"

"Oh, right, so Allison is your new friend. Got it. She's the one who left all those messages on the machine the other night."

"What messages?" I ask, alarmed.

"You didn't get those? Let's see, it was that night you went out with Aunt Rusty. Was that Saturday night? Yeah, you went to that poetry bash thing."

"Poetry slam! Dad, how could you not tell me about the messages?"

He shrugs. "I don't know. I just thought you got them."

I look at my mom. "Don't look at me," she says. "I never heard them."

I go into the kitchen, leaving them to argue about who dropped the ball on the parenting skills this time. I press the messages button on the answering machine. It says there are twelve saved messages and starts playing them.

"Hi, Clare, it's Allison. Look, I think we could have some fun at this party tonight. A few laughs anyway. I get why you don't want to go, but you can be my date. Get that party dress out of the mothballs and I'll pick you up at eight. Call me. Bye."

<beep>

"Hey, Clare, me again. It's seven-thirty and I'm leaving soon. Do me a favour and call me even if you don't want to go. I just want to talk to you, okay? Bye."

<beep>

"Hey, me again. This is the last time I'm calling. I mean it. Call me back. If you don't, I'm just going to go to that party and you'll be sorry. Bye."

<beep>

"Okay, really, I mean it. Last chance for romance ... really. Bye."

I picture myself sitting in front of my therapist in twenty years explaining that my dad ruined my life because he doesn't know how to work an answering machine. He can run a corporation from his briefcase, but pass on a message? Forget about it.

It's too late to call Allison and say, "Hey, I got your message and ..."

Too much water has gone under the bridge; that ship has sailed; my goose is cooked. I decide that the best possible way to deal with this is to approach Allison at school the next day, tell her what happened and just see where it goes from there.

Later, when I'm staring up at the ceiling in my bedroom, reviewing life's latest catastrophe, a chill runs through me when I think about the fortune teller and how she told me that the misunderstanding was partly my fault. In fact, come to think of it, a lot of things she told me that night have come true. Which reminds me of the three witches in *Macbeth*. Macbeth listens to them and gets himself into a horrible mess. I try to remember what else that crazy woman told me. Didn't she say what's broken shall be fixed? Does that mean I'm in charge of fixing it or will it fix itself? And what about this curse my mom told me about? Should I be afraid for my life?

Elsie is lying on the carpet next to my bed. She's having one of her cat-chasing dreams where her paws move and she woofs quietly. I shake her and she wakes with a start. She looks around and rolls over. I give her belly a scratch.

"Elsie, help me out here. What am I going to say tomorrow?"

Elsie puts her paw on my hand, which either means "Scratch me some more right there" or "Don't worry, you'll think of something." A dog's life is so uncomplicated.

About the Author

Yvonne Prinz was born in Edmonton, Alberta. She now lives in the San Francisco Bay area, where she and her husband founded a chain of independent record stores. *Still There, Clare* is her first novel, and the first in a series of books about Clare. Yvonne still consults with her imaginary friend on a regular basis and enlisted her help in writing these books.

www.stillthereclare.com